Malicious Love

By

Maggie Snodgrass

PublishAmerica
Baltimore

First printing

ISBN: 1-60474-862-1
PUBLISHED BY PUBLISHAMERICA, LLLP
www.publishamerica.com
Baltimore

Printed in the United States of America

To Margo, Michael, Mary and John…thanks, kids!

Chapter One

It could have been early morning or maybe evening when she woke up. Only darkness could be seen outside the window and in her room one soft light glowed. She opened her eyes and tried to see through a blinding mist that coated her vision. Carefully she rubbed her eyes until she could make out her surroundings.

A hospital room. Stark and crisp, the room smelled of disinfectant. Slowly she pulled herself up on the bed and reached for the nurse call button. Immediately a voice came over a small intercom at her bedside and asked what she wanted.

"I...ah...just woke up. Could you tell me where I am?" she asked quietly.

"You're in the Lewiston County Hospital miss," the tinny voice said and then was quiet for a moment. "I'm going to contact your doctor. I think he's still in the hospital. In the meantime, just lay back quietly. I'll send an aide down to bring you something to eat, you must be hungry..."

The voice broke off leaving her alone again in the quiet, sterile room. She raised the top of the bed and lay back against the snowy pillows. Outside her room she heard the hurried footsteps of someone but they went on by. Her head hurt and she raised her hand to her forehead and found it covered with a bandage. There must have been an accident of some kind, but what?

Smiling cheerfully a young, round woman approached her door and knocked softly. She was dressed in a white uniform, her pants spotted with greasy stains. Her thin dark hair was pulled back into a hurried bun that couldn't quite hold it. Wisps of oily hair framed her round face.

"Hi! I was told you wanted something to eat. My name is Gail. Here's your supper tray," she sat the tray on the bedside table and rolled it to her. "You ain't got any ice water sweetie, I'll be right back. You just lay still."

Cautiously she lifted the lid to the dinner tray and stared at the unrecognizable food beneath it. Poking at it with a fork she decided she wasn't really hungry after all. Putting the lid back on the plate, she pushed the table away. Laying back again she continued to stare out at the dark window.

Gail bounced back into the room. First she filled the water glass and sat it close to the tray. Lifting the cover she looked at her questionably. "Ain't you gonna eat honey? It's not bad, really, the pot roast. The spuds is a little soggy, but the meat and veggies is good. The pie is real good, you should try it..."

She turned her head away when the aide offered her a bite.

"Well...if'n you ain't gonna eat it...hate to see good food go to waste..." the aide began to stuff her face with gusto. Around a bite of meat she smiled. "You ain't told me your name honey, what is it?"

She looked at the nurses' aide and frowned. What was her name? A thought had been nagging her since she'd wakened but she couldn't bring it forward...She closed her eyes.

Nothing...

Rubbing her forehead she muttered quietly, "I...I...can't remember..."

Heavy footsteps were coming down the hall. "Ah shit honey, don't tell no one I et your meal, okay? I'll get my butt in a real grinder if'n they catch me doin' that agin." Wiping her face on the back of her hand she quickly gathered up the tray. As the white jacketed doctor pushed open the door Gail said in a loud voice, "You et pretty well, honey, considerin'. Maybe you'll be able to do more tomorrow."

Nodding quietly at the doctor she left the room, the dinner tray with her.

Walking to the bed the doctor took her wrist, "Good evening. How are you feeling tonight?" He was tall, graying at the temples. The dark rimmed glasses made him look more stern than his voice sounded. His face was kind, lined with years of worry. "I'm Doctor Priestly," he took out a penlight and shone it in her eyes. "I've been waiting for you to wake up so we could introduce ourselves. Can you tell me your name?"

"I can't seem to remember..." she whispered hoarsely. "How long have I been here?"

The doctor patted her hand and smiled. "You've been here since this morning. It's about seven o'clock in the evening now. You've got a nasty bump on the head." He took a chair beside her, "You've obviously been in an accident, your clothes were wet and muddy like you may have been in the river. The Clearwater isn't far from here but the sheriff wasn't able to find a vehicle. That's to be expected if it went into the river as it's quite swollen this time of year. It's fast moving and treacherous. The sheriff is puzzled as to how you could have gotten out of a car without being swept under and drowned." He pulled a pen from his pocket and began to write on a chart. He rubbed his eyes tiredly.

"Your identification wasn't with you. Can you tell me anything about yourself?"

For a moment she sat quietly then she shook her head. "No, nothing. Everything is blank."

He made another note on her chart. "Not to worry. I'm sure as soon as the swelling goes down everything will come back to you. In the meantime, you're safe and in pretty good shape. Try to rest. If you need to get up to go to the bathroom, buzz the nurse. I don't want you falling and possibly bumping your head again. I'll see you tomorrow morning."

He stood and smiled down at her. Patting her hand he again told her, "Try not to worry. It's not unusual for a head injury such as yours to create temporary amnesia...Get some rest now."

With the same hurried steps he left the room. Everything again became silent and she lay looking out the darkened window. She may have dozed for a while but woke with a start at a soft voice at her elbow.

"Sorry," he apologized and smiled at her. "I…ah…just wanted to check on you. I'm the one that found you this morning. I work for the county road department…" he was tall, dark haired and very handsome. His blue, blue eyes seemed to cut to the very soul of her and she had to look away from their hypnotic gaze. Gently he stuck out his hand, " I'm Louis Sammons. You don't remember me huh?"

She shook her head and tried not to look into those eyes. "I' m sorry. The doctor says I have a bad bump on the head and once the swelling goes down I should be able to remember…things."

Nodding he looked around the room. "Do you need anything? I mean, well, I sort of feel responsible for you, finding you and all that…silly kind of…but anyway, I have a friend that's about your size. I can ask her if she has any clothes you can use."

Blushing she looked away to the window again. "I don't know. I have no way of paying for anything, at least not right now."

"Don't worry about it," he patted her arm. She recoiled from him. His touch had an odd effect on her. Immediately her mind filled with a suffocating, choking sensation.

"What is it?" he asked. "Did you remember something?"

"I don't know," she said, closing her eyes. "I guess I'm really tired. Would you mind coming back some other time."

"Oh…oh sure. I'll try to stop in tomorrow." He walked to the door then turned back toward her. "Don't be afraid to remember," he said softly as he left the room.

Immediately the door opened again and the night nurse came in. As the nurse attached the blood pressure cup to her arm, she looked up at the nurse. "Do you know that man that was just in here?"

The nurse pulled the stethoscope from her ears. "What? Did you say something?"

She repeated the question.

"What man is that? I didn't see anyone." The nurse replaced the stethoscope and returned to taking her blood pressure.

She frowned...How could the nurse have missed him? She came in the same door just as he was leaving the room. Maybe the nurse was distracted but she would have almost run into him as he slipped out the door. Maybe the nurse was overworked, in a hurry, maybe she wasn't completely aware of what was going on around her.

The nurse checked the water in the pitcher. "Do you need to use the bathroom while I'm here?"

She shook her head no.

"Okay, but if you decide later you need to, be sure to buzz us. The doctor has ordered you are not to get out of bed unassisted." Pulling her blankets straight over her, the nurse turned down the light and left the room.

She lay in the dark for a while thinking about the man Louis. He had seemed genuinely concerned about her. Odd that he would have slipped away without being noticed. It was really too late for visitors, how had he even gotten into the hospital?

Drowsily she closed her eyes. There were a lot of questions she needed answered. Why was she here in Lewiston County? Did she live in this area? Surely someone would have recognized her if that were true. Was she visiting someone, family perhaps ? Again if that were true someone would have been looking for her. Her head swam dizzily from the unanswered questions and it hurt. Turning on her side she sighed deeply, closed her eyes and slept.

The light was bright and hurt her eyes when she opened them the next morning. Across the room a very young nurses' aide was placing clean bedding on a chair. She was blonde, slender, and very petite. Looking over at her she smiled, "Good morning, ma'am. Are you ready to take a shower?"

"What time is it?" she asked.

"It's about eight o'clock," the aide answered as she carefully pulled the blankets back. "The charge nurse decided to let you sleep in. I'm to help you to the bathroom...ready?"

Carefully she lowered her feet to the floor. It was a short walk to the bathroom but she felt dizzy and weak and was thankful someone was there to steady her. In the shower the water cascaded over her in a heavenly spray. It felt glorious. Dressed in a clean gown she slowly walked back to the bed.

"Your breakfast is here, still. It's probably cold. Would you like me to have it warmed for you?" the cheerful aide asked as she helped her get comfortable...

Under the lid they found cold cereal and a dish of fruit along with a mass of yellow stuff that was probably egg substitute, two pieces of limp toast and a small pot of jelly. She smiled at the aide. "The cereal and fruit will be fine, thank-you." Nodding the girl left.

Nibbling at the food she managed to get most of it down when the door swung open again. Thinking it was the aide back to collect the tray she smiled, "I ate what I could. I guess I'm not that hungry."

His voice was as soft this day as it had been the night before. "You'll never get better if you don't keep up your strength. You need to force yourself to eat."

There he was again, his blue eyes boring into hers and she had to quickly look away.

"How are you feeling this morning?" he asked quietly and slowly approached her bed.

She felt fear welling up inside her, unreasonable, uncontrollable, raw and intense. The closer he got to her the more intense the feeling. She opened her mouth to say something to him and felt a scream erupt.

Immediately the room was filled with white clothed figures. A nurse, an orderly and the tiny aide were peering at her with varying frowns and looks of concern.

"What happened miss?" the charge nurse asked solemnly. "Why did you scream?"

"There...was...a...man...in my room," she was finally able to squeeze past the constriction in her throat.

"A man?" the orderly said softly. "It's Sunday. There hasn 't been anyone around here this morning, not even the doctors. Are you sure you didn't see one of us near your door?"

She shook her head violently. "No! There was a man in here. He...was here last night too..." she put her hand to her head and shook it. " He said he worked for the road department..." they stared at her not able to understand. Finally in desperation she told them, "please, please could you just leave me alone? I don't feel well."

The head nurse chased everyone out of her room, except the little aide. "Janet will stay with you for a while. Try to rest. Dr. Priestly will be here soon."

Laying back against her pillow she forced herself to breath normally. Quietly the nurse explained to the aide, "....the patient could be hallucinating. If she shows any further symptoms notify the desk immediately."

Finally her heart quieted and she felt herself becoming calm. What about the handsome stranger made her feel so terrified? She could think of nothing he did that could make her feel such a strong emotion. His touch had been gentle last night, tender, but it had sent such terror through her that she couldn't stand the thought of him being close to her again.

"Are you feeling better now?" Janet said softly. She had been sitting quietly in a chair beside the bed.

She smiled at the tiny woman. "I'm sorry. You must think I'm some kind of a mental case."

Janet smiled back. "No. Not at all. Actually I'm grateful for the chance to sit down. We've been short handed all morning. This is the first break I've had all day."

"Tell me about yourself," she asked quietly, hoping to fill her thoughts with friendly conversation.

"Well, my name is Janet Napp. I'm nineteen years old, soon to be twenty...I've been working as a nurses' aide for almost two years now...I graduated from high school and went right into a program that will allow me to get my nurses' cap. All day I work, evenings I go to school. I have a little boy, eighteen months old. His grandma watches him while I work and go to school."

She smiled tenderly at the young woman sitting primly in the chair with her hands in her lap…She seemed timid, meek, mousey. "What did you say your name is?"

"Umm….Janet Napp." After a moment she said, "The doctors say you have amnesia. You really can't remember anything at all?"

She shook her head.

"That must be horrible for you," Janet said softly. She stood up and walked to the window. "I couldn't go on every day except for the smile of my little boy. I don't think I could live without his face in my mind all day to keep me going. Would you like to see his picture?"

She nodded…Janet pulled out a small picture of a beautiful little boy. He was smiling a toothless smile and holding his arms up as if to be picked up.

"Isn't he a love? He's such a good baby too. Even my mom remarks how good he is."

"Where's the daddy?" she asked and immediately wished she hadn't.

"He….ah….took off before he found out Frankie was on the way. I don't know where he is. I'm a single mom. My mother has a hard time handling that. She's from a strict Christian background, Southern Baptist. She says that God has forgiven me….but I don't think she has."

Janet 's head drooped then and it wasn't hard to see the pain, her heart ached for the girl.

Suddenly the intercom crackled, "Janet are you still there?"

Janet stepped to the side of the bed, "Yes'm. You told me to stay with the lady."

"How is Jane Doe doing? Has she settled down?" the voice asked.

"I….I think so."

"Good. I need you in room 23. Mr. Anderson has soiled his bed again. Grab some sheets and head down there right away."

"Isn't room 23 Nick's room?"

"I know, I know, Nick just went home sick. Don't argue with me young woman! I said get down to room 23 right away!" the voice growled from the small box.

The hurt expression filled Janet's eyes again as she tried to smile. " I guess I'd better go. I'll try to stop by later, if that's all right with you."

"I'd like that," she answered. "Good luck, honey..."

It was quiet in the room again. She lay back against her bed and tried to bring any kind of a memory up from her mind. Nothing. Lifting the mirror in her bedside table she stared at the strangely familiar face looking back at her.

Almost black hair with touches of gray told her she must be close to forty. Dark brown eyes reflected the emptiness she felt. Her skin was smooth, only a hint of crows-feet, and her teeth were perfect. At least she had taken care of herself. Sighing she closed the mirror and turned again to the window.

Watching a small bird light at her window, then fly away she thought again of Janet. She was as timid as that little bird. The girl was pathetic in a lot of ways. She apparently had low self-esteem, no self confidence and didn't know how to stand up for herself. At work it was obvious she was unable to stand up to anyone, and she imagined Janet was pretty much the same way at home.

Janet 's problems seem to help her feel less uncomfortable about her own. At least it was something to think about. She could remember this morning and last night and that was the extent of her life memories. It was spooky and disorienting...How could a person survive without bases to touch, anchors to hold you? Surely this wouldn't last much longer. Surely the swelling would go down soon and her memories would come flooding back to her!

Doctor Priestly marched into her room. His worried frown looked over his patient and turned into a quick smile. "Want to tell me what the ruckus was about earlier? Did you remember something that frightened you?"

Turning away from the doctor's gaze she shook her head, "I don't know Dr. Priestly. It was odd. A man was here and then I felt such an overwhelming fear....every pore of my body was afraid. I could almost taste it."

He nodded solemnly, "Afraid? Of what? Did he threaten you or try to harm you? Did he suggest something that made you think you were in danger?"

Again she shook her head. "No. Nothing like that. It was his eyes....sort of. His eyes were hypnotic and seemed to look right into the heart of me. And there was something more....I can't explain."

Dr. Priestly sat down gingerly on the edge of her bed. His gentle hand covered hers. "I guess I don't understand but I'm not surprised. From what I have read, amnesia is a tricky thing and to be quite frank I don't know much about it. Actually you are my first amnesia patient. I'm thinking if you haven't recovered your memory in just a few days, I'm going to call in a specialist. Would that be all right with you?"

She nodded...Yes, that would be a good idea. She simply had to know who she was, what had happened, and why she was here. And she needed to know who the stranger was that caused her such fear. Where had he come from? Why did he frighten her so?

Too many questions, she decided.

The doctor stood, "I'm going to order a light sedative for you. I want you to rest as much as you can." He scribbled something on her chart. "The nurse will be in in a few minutes to give you a shot."

Closing her eyes she heard the gentle whoosh of her door as the doctor let himself out. The nurse came in a few minutes later and she felt the sting of the hypo. Almost immediately she felt her body begin to relax and as she drifted off to sleep she saw again those blue eyes smiling at her.

Chapter Two

It was going to be a long slow recovery. Physical therapy was needed to restore her balance and strength. As the days slowly rolled into weeks she became panicked at the thought of never knowing who she was. Dr. Priestly decided they'd waited long enough. The second week of her recovery he called in a specialist.

The psychiatrist called in was a pinched faced man that looked out at her from thick glasses with black frames. He was short and somewhat disheveled. He said very little to her in their sessions, as if he were waiting for her to suddenly speak a foreign language or do something spectacular. He made her feel nervous and uneasy.

Finally, after a week, Dr. Langer's strange behavior made her turn on him.

"Why are you looking at me like that?" she demanded.

"I'm sorry," he wheezed, "looking at you? How?"

"Like I'm some kind of a freak. I'm not going to grow a third eye or suddenly start yelling in German. I'm just a normal human being that can't remember who I am or where I'm from and I can't say you're doing anything to help me remember!" Her voice had risen in volume until she was close to yelling.

Pulling his glasses from his thin face he rubbed them on his shirt sleeve. "I do apologize, my dear. I guess I have been a little rude, I don't mean to be. Amnesia fascinates me as every case is different. Actual full blown amnesia is rare and quite tragic. A person cannot remember from one moment to the next what has happened. Such extreme cases are not usually from a blow to the head, but rather from disease or an accident that destroys the part of the mind that holds short term memory. There are two kinds of memory, short term and long term. There is no recovery from a total loss of short term memory and coping with the loss is devastating. You, however, have not that kind of problem. You have evidently suffered a blow to the head just over your long term memory center. Plus, I suspect, you have had an emotional trauma. Once we figure out what the trauma was, we may be able to help you."

She blinked at the little man. How had he come to that conclusion when he'd barely spoken to her? She sat looking at him quizzically. "How do you know all that?"

Putting his glasses back on the thin man stood up, "Years of experience, careful study of your records, and some wild guessing." He smiled then and left the room.

Frowning she sat back against the cushions of her chair. They were having a session in the solarium; an area of light colored casual chairs and indoor plants. It was a comfortable room and usually put patients at ease. But she wasn't sure if she liked Dr. Langer. There was something about him that felt....false. Laying back against the chair she let the gentle sunlight warm her face. Behind her she could hear the soft shuffle of a patient as he made his way down the hall to an important appointment.

Healing...All around her there was healing going on. In the three weeks since she'd awakened in the hospital bed, patients had come into her life and left within days. Some had gone on to other centers and others had gone home.

Home. Somewhere there had to be an address that belonged to her.

Janet had suggested the FBI be called to investigate her past. Strangely enough, her specialist fought the idea. "It would be better if you remembered on your own."

She had insisted and an agent was called. She'd been fingerprinted in hopes of finding something out about herself. They were still awaiting the results. If she had no record anywhere, or had never been fingerprinted, chances are they'd not be able to help her either. But, it was a place to start and now all that was left was the waiting.

A cat scan showed the swelling had gone down. There was no apparent permanent damage...Her specialist then decided it must be an emotional trauma that was holding back her memory. But, without a clue as to who she was, why she was there, and what had happened, there was no lead as to where to start looking for the reason.

It was like a gigantic loop. All the paths seemed to be interconnected, folding back on themselves. When you thought you were headed in a new direction, you were actually doubling back on yourself. She ended each day more frustrated and confused than that morning.

Hypnosis was tried, several times, but the doctor could get no farther than the block she had put up against the memory that had so terrified her. Was the blue-eyed man somehow involved? Was that why his presence sent her into spasms of fear? She asked those questions of herself often.

"I'm not sure how much longer I can handle this....nothingness...." she complained to Dr. Langer the next day. "I'm thinking I must get on with something....anything. I can't live in the hospital for the rest of my life."

"You're right," Dr. Langer agreed. He held a large manila envelope in his hands. "This arrived this morning. It's the results of the FBI search. I haven't opened it yet. Shall we?"

Handing her the envelope he took a seat across from her. For a moment the envelope laid in her hands before she realized what the doctor was saying. Her life was about to be given back to her. What if there was nothing in the envelope? What would she do then?

Slowly she tore open the end. Inside was a thick report, stapled at the top left-hand corner. Reading the words on the pages she smiled, "My name is Lisa Miller...I live in North Vancouver, Washington. I am a writer by trade, live alone in an apartment alongside the Columbia River and was reported missing by my agent, Beth Mosher three weeks ago."

The doctor watched her closely, "Does any of this sound familiar?"

Lisa shook her head, "No. Nothing. My mind is still blank."

"Then I would suggest we try another hypnosis session. If that doesn't help, you might want to consider returning to your apartment. Sometimes being around familiar surroundings jars loose memories." The doctor again pulled his glasses from his face and polished them on his shirt sleeve. "We can contact your agent and see if she is willing to come here to drive you home. You should probably have someone stay with you for a while....at least until you have your feet under you again...."

Immediately she thought of Janet. Janet had said she wished she could get away from Lewiston...Over the last several weeks they had become close. Thinking of the picture of the angelic child Lisa wondered if she could handle having a small child around her all the time. Was her home safe for a baby? There was no way for her to know...

The agent was contacted later that morning. She sounded thankful that Lisa was alive and more or less whole, "What in God's name were you doing in Idaho Lisa? We've all been worried sick about you."

Lisa was unable to answer Beth's questions but her friend just chuckled, "Oh hell Lisa, it doesn't matter what you're doing there. I'll be glad to come and get you and bring you home. You are more than just a client you know, you and I have been friends for over twelve years." Beth quickly made arrangements to come for her. It would be an eight hour drive but she would be there the next afternoon.

As soon as Beth hung up, Lisa asked Janet to come to her room. Explaining to the young woman what she wanted, Lisa asked her if she would like to move to Vancouver with her.

Eyes wide with excitement Janet turned to Lisa, "Can I bring Frankie with me ? Will we have a room of our own?"

"Of course your son can come. From what I understand I have a huge two bedroom apartment. You and your little boy can have a room to yourselves. I'd pay you a wage and you could still go to school there, if you like. Beth tells me there are a lot of night school programs available that even provide childcare...After a while you can find a job that suits you and a place of your own. What do you think Janet? Are you interested?"

"Am I interested? This is an answer to a prayer!" Janet leaned over the bed and gave Lisa a hug. "When will we leave?"

Lisa explained her friend would be picking them up the next day, probably in the afternoon...Frowning slightly Janet told her she would meet them in the parking lot. "I'll be at the hospital door, waiting. I'm not sure how my mother will handle this....she might....oh well....I'll be there! Thank you so much!"

That evening Dr. Langer insisted they try hypnosis one more time. It was evening and the room where he started the session was dimly lit. Lisa tried to relax, to listen to his words, but her mind was too full of the coming day. Finally Dr. Priestly was called in. In quiet consultation the two doctors decided to try a drug induced hypnosis.

Lisa frowned. Why? She didn't like chemicals being pumped into her body. Why was it so important for her to be put under now? She listened as Dr. Priestly ordered the medication. A friendly nurse entered and asked to see her arm. With a quick prick the needle was inserted. In moments Lisa felt herself swept away into a dreamy state.

It felt like one moment she went to sleep and the next someone was telling her to wake up. Blinking she looked around the room. Only Dr. Langer was there. He smiled at her and told her to be careful sitting up.

"Did it do any good?" Lisa asked and raised her head carefully.

Shaking his head he held out his hand to help her sit up. "Like before, nothing...I was hoping once you knew your name it would jar something loose on the subconscious level, but it didn't. Once you get home I recommend you continue therapy...I will give you several names of colleagues you might want to contact."

It was hard sleeping that night. Every time sleep almost found her Lisa would think about meeting Beth the next day. Would seeing someone from her past set loose the flood of memories, or would it be more subtle? Would she remember one by one things that finally put her life back together? The thought tantalized her and kept her awake.

Morning came early. Lisa was awake and showered long before the rest of the hospital. She dressed in a silky sweat suit someone had given her. Janet did not come in this morning. She was probably home, packing and getting ready to leave.

Lisa kept looking at the clock. Beth had said she would be there by three o' clock. Barely seven, it was hard to stand the wait.

"Good morning Lisa."

His voice came from behind her as she stood at the window. It was soft and kind, and immediately she felt the fear closing in on her. Fighting against the terror she turned slowly, determined to look him straight in the eye.

"Who are you?" she demanded in a trembling voice, "What are you doing here?" She steadied herself against the window sill. "Why do you keep coming back?"

"I heard you were leaving. I also heard you've found out who you are…I'm Louis, remember? Louis Sammons, the guy who found you and brought you to the hospital. I just wanted to say good-bye and I'm happy you found your roots. I also wanted to ask you if you remember anything about that morning." His eyes bored through hers until she could no longer meet their gaze.

Turning away from him she answered, "I know my name is Lisa Miller and that I live in Vancouver, Washington. I am a writer. Other than that there is nothing…I remember no one from my past…." she turned again to look at him, determined he would no longer have this strange hold on her. The room was empty…

Cold chills chased up her back and suddenly her legs were too weak to hold her. Stumbling to a chair she sat down until the shaking stopped.

Beth was right on time. But when the heavy set fifty year old woman entered the room, there was nothing. No sudden remembering of days past; no sudden memories; no recollection of the thirty-eight years of life she'd lived. Beth introduced herself as if there hadn't been twelve years of history shared by the two women.

Disappointed Lisa sat down on the bed. Beth looked around the room.

"Are you all packed kiddo?"

Lisa nodded.

"Where's the little gal you hired to come home with you?" Beth asked.

"She'll meet us out front. She had to go home and get some things for herself and her little boy." Lisa picked up the one very small bag of things she was taking home with her and tried to smile. "Let' s go see if Janet is ready."

Signing out of the hospital took several minutes. Every paper she signed, Beth read over carefully.

"Kiddo, I think you just signed away most of the royalty checks from your last book," she smiled half seriously.

Scanning the parking lot Lisa looked for Janet. At first she was afraid they were early or the girl had changed her mind. As Beth and Lisa approached a large late model town car, Janet suddenly came out from the side of the building and half ran to where they were standing. She carried only the child without more than a few blankets against the cool May wind. There was a small travel bag, but no suitcase, nothing to show the girl planned on leaving. Beth opened the car doors and the girl and her child quickly settled into the back seat, pulling the door shut behind her and locking it.

Lisa and Beth exchanged startled glances. Sticking her head inside the car Lisa asked, "Is this Frankie?" When Janet nodded Beth asked, "Don't you have to have an infant seat for him to ride in a car?"

Janet stared at them for a moment, "My mom and I don't own a car and usually travel by bus. I don't have a car seat for Frankie. Can't I just hold him on my lap while we travel?"

Beth shook her head. "Sorry dearie. The law says we have to have a seat for the little rascal. Hospitals usually sell them. Let's dash back inside and check with the information desk."

The young mother ducked her head and almost whimpered, "Can't we find something on the way? Can't we get started first?"

Looking over at her friend Lisa felt a shudder go through her. What was going on? Why was Janet so anxious to get away?

Taking a seat in the front, Beth quickly climbed into the car too. Looking over the back of the seat Lisa looked Janet in the eyes. "I don't know what is wrong here, but I think you had better explain."

Janet started to make some excuse for wanting to leave right away, then turned her pale face away from Lisa. Finally when she realized the two women were not going to start the car she began to talk.

As she had told Lisa, she lived with her widowed mother, just she and Frankie. But it was more than just her mother watching the baby, as she had told Lisa. Her mother had taken over complete care of the child. Janet was not allowed to do anything with or for the baby. Her mother told her she was an unfit mother and couldn't be trusted to raise the child correctly. If she even wanted to see him or be near him she had to do as her mother insisted. Today she had sneaked him out of the house while her mother napped.

"There was no other place for me to go when I was expecting. Mother told me I could stay with her, but I had to go to work, immediately after the baby was born or I would be put out of the house. For the last eighteen months I have only seen Frankie for maybe two hours a day. Sometimes at night I can hear him fussing, but she keeps him in her room and won't let me have anything to do with him. It has been pure hell...." the tears started then. After a moment she got herself under control again, "My mother will call the sheriff and if we're spotted they'll try to take Frankie back to her."

Beth turned to Lisa. Under her breath she asked, "Are you sure you know what you're doing?"

Lisa nodded. Wordlessly Beth started the car and pulled away from the hospital. Within minutes she pulled in front of a large department store. "Stay put," she told Lisa and Janet. "I'll only be a minute."

Ten minutes later she was back with a child's seat. Quickly the women figured out how to install the seat and had Frankie secured in it. Within the hour they had traveled far from Lewiston and were well on their way back to Washington state. Only then did the three begin to relax. Frankie and his mother were safe. At least for the moment.

It was a barren drive. The countryside was raw and rugged and filled with very little scenery. Miles of straight roadway stretched before them with hardly an occasional house to distract them from the emptiness. Occasional rain drops splattered against the windshield as small storms hurried over them, but for the most part the sky stayed blue and clear.

While driving the two women in front talked quietly. In the back Janet and the boy slept soundly. Lisa asked Beth a thousand questions about herself. Beth answered each one patiently. Two hours later they finally came to a small town.

Stopping for gas gave everyone a chance to stretch their legs. Standing outside the car Lisa looked around. There wasn't much to the town; a post office, a grocery store, a gas station, a small café, and an antique store, but there was something almost déjà vu about it. Pulling her sun glasses from her face she stared at the antique store. As if in a trance she walked to the front door. It was locked. The sign said the store was closed on Mondays and Tuesdays and all holidays. The feeling of familiarity was strongest here.

Beth came over to where Lisa was standing, "What is it kiddo? Have you remembered something?"

Rather than try to explain the strange sensations she was feeling she shook her head sadly, "No. I just wanted to see what was in the store. Do I like antiques ?"

Beth snorted, "Like them! You're apartment is like a damn museum. You have these beautiful old dishes all over the place. I don't know how you plan on having a little guy around all those treasures of yours. You and Janet better plan on a quick baby proofing when you get to your apartment."

Lisa blushed. Although she liked Janet and the little boy was charming, she wondered if her moving in was really such a good idea. The secret she'd revealed while in the car had unnerved her, somewhat. What did she know about Janet anyway ?

But something made her trust the girl. She was meck, unable to stand up for herself and maybe that made Lisa feel sorry for her, but she was willing to take the chance.

About the time the trio was ready to head back into the car a voice started calling from across the street, "Yoo hoo! Lisa Miller! Is that really you?"

A tall thin woman dressed in a fashionable pants suit waved and hurried across the street..."It is you! How are you? Wait until I tell Harriet about seeing you...You know, I love that book of yours and I treasure the sentiment you wrote in it for me. I'm the envy of everyone in our literary club. Say. Would you consider signing a few more books....I can run into the store and get a half dozen copies right away...."

Beth stepped over to Lisa's side and shook her head. "Not today, sorry...Lisa is recuperating from an accident and we're kind of in a hurry. Excuse us, ma'am. Come on Lisa we need to get going."

The tall woman grimaced with embarrassment and started muttering as she walked away "....never did hold with her ways...." ". .kind of uppity.... "

Settling into the car Lisa turned toward the window, "I think you just cost me a fan, Beth."

Beth snorted and started the car, "I think you can stand the loss."

They rode along silently for a while. In the back seat Janet and Frankie played quietly...The baby was a good traveler and did not fuss. From the bag at her feet Janet produced bottles, small crackers, jars of baby food and diapers as the need arose...At least she hadn't come away completely unprepared.

Across the Idaho, Oregon boarder they began to see more and more homes. Small towns began to crop up. Finally they pulled onto the highway leading west across the state of Oregon. They stopped at an old motel-café in Bigs to buy supper. Taking a seat next to a large window they looked up in surprise when a TV newscast across the room suddenly flashed an AMBER alert with Janet's picture. Listening carefully they were able to hear, "....the young woman and her son have disappeared under suspicious circumstances. The boy is about eighteen months old, blonde haired and blue eyes. Anyone seeing the two are to contact the authorities right away...."

Janet 's eyes were wide with fright. There was no one else in the room. The waitress had stepped to the back to bring them water glasses and menus. Quietly Beth handed Janet a pair of sunglasses, "Hand Frankie to Lisa and head out to the car. Put those sunglasses on and act like you're not feeling well. Don't run. Walk. Lisa and I will order a couple of sandwiches to go and join you."

Nodding silently she lifted the baby from her lap and handed him to Lisa. Slipping on the sunglasses she walked out the door. Frankie sat in Lisa's lap staring at her but not fussing.

The waitress came to the table and watched as Janet walked away.

"Is the young lady all right? She seemed real upset about something."

"Car sick," Beth replied. "Poor thing. My friend here and I would like a BLT each, to go. And a small dish of applesauce for the little guy. Maybe some pudding too, if you have it."

"What a cute baby!" the waitress exclaimed. "What' s his name?"

Frankie looked at her and smiled while he chortled his baby talk.

"His name is Leonard. He's my grandson." Lisa said quietly..."We're kind of in a hurry. Would you also bring a turkey sandwich and a large 7-up for the mama? She may get hungry later."

"Oh sure, no problem," the waitress scribbled their order down and smiled again at the baby. "We'll have your order up real quick like..."

As soon as the waitress left Beth whispered, "I think we'd better make this a quick stop and get the heck out of here. That newscaster may make that broadcast again and someone might make the connection." Then in a quieter whisper she asked, "Are you sure you want to take this kid home with you ?"

Lisa nodded. "It'll be all right. Let me handle this."

"You always were stubborn...." she heard Beth mutter.

The rest of the trip was uneventful. It was very late when they pulled up in front of a modern looking apartment building. Beth locked the car and let them into the building with her key. "There's a nice garage for the tenants and their guests, in the basement. I don't park there. The super is holding another set of keys for you and will bring them by in the morning. The keys to your car are in the apartment on a table by the front door. I'll walk up with you and let you in. You're on the third floor, back side of the apartment building overlooking the river."

Silently they walked to the elevator. Plush carpets cushioned their feet. A watchman nodded as they passed him on his rounds. Approaching the elevator Lisa felt something, a slight stirring, but nothing came from it.

Following Beth's lead they walked to apartment 31 and waited while the door was unlocked. Inside the door Beth flipped a switch that illuminated a showplace room...

Slowly Lisa walked into her home. The front room stretched before her. Huge glass windows looked out across the inky strip of river below. Lights could be seen from the many ships and boats as they cruised the waterway. Along the tops of special shelves, the bookcase, and the china hutch were marvelous old glassware from the early 1900s. Colorful pictures covered the walls. Overstuffed furniture and richly woven rugs combined the colors of the glassware. To the left a large dining room could be seen. Oaken chairs and a table with a large kitchen just beyond that. To the right was a dark hallway.

"That is your bedroom back there," Beth pointed Lisa down the hall. "Janet your room and bathroom is back here. If you'll come with me you can put Frankie down." The baby's head lay against his mother's shoulder and wobbled a bit as Janet followed to her new room.

Slowly walking down the short hallway Lisa turned on the light just inside the door. She looked up in surprise when a large yellow cat jumped from the bed to the floor and walked slowly toward her. Beth had told her the cat's name was Topaz...She held out her hand and called to the animal. The cat stopped in his tracks, looked up at her, and hissed. Scrambling by her it disappeared into the kitchen...Shaken by the cat's behavior Lisa stood in the doorway for a moment.

When her wits came back to her she looked around the large room. Inside the door she found a queen size bed with richly colored comforter and pillows done up in golds, greens, blues and purples. Beyond the bedroom was a door leading to her bathroom...

All of the fixtures in the bathroom were color coordinated with the master bedroom, right down to the rugs on the floor and the shower curtain.

Smiling inwardly she walked back to the front room. Beth was sitting on the couch stroking Topaz. "The girl is putting Frankie to bed. I think she's a little bit dazed with all this. She sure is a puzzlement, that one. I can't tell if she's being truthful with us or not." She put the cat down and stood up.

"Do you like your place? You decorated it yourself when you moved in about seven years ago."

"It's a little overwhelming. I don't know where anything is, but I like it!" Lisa fingered a thick purple bowl on an end table. It was striking with its facetted cut sides and the deepness of its color.

Yawning and stretching Beth excused herself. "I'm awfully tired, kiddo...I didn't get much sleep last night. I'll be back early tomorrow and we can talk all you want then, ok? I'll bring the kid's car seat up when I come back in the morning."

Lisa nodded, "Thanks for everything Beth. I really appreciate it. I don't know how I'll ever repay you."

Beth snorted her funny little laugh. "Get to writing again kiddo. That's how you'll repay me."

Chapter Three

It's like a treasure hunt, Lisa told herself as she opened another drawer in a cabinet. She never knew what she was going to find. Each drawer, cupboard, closet she opened might be the one that held the key to her memories. Systematically she searched every box, every nook and cranny looking for that key. Nothing worked. Her mind was still a blank.

Sometimes she felt like an intruder in this lavishly beautiful apartment. Standing at the glass window looking over the river she couldn't help but feel displaced, lost. This just didn't feel like the kind of place she would have wanted to live in.

The kitchen, she discovered, was set up for gourmet cooking. Could she cook? Opening the cupboards and staring at the equipment stored in them, she doubted it. She was lost in this glorious work place. Janet just smiled and took over, she was the good cook. They wouldn't starve.

Beth told her, she'd never been able to cook. "You could burn water....all of your meals were either eaten out or brought in. That fancy kitchen of yours was strictly for show....or for someone visiting who liked to cook. Sometimes a sleepover guest turned out to be a chef....if you know what I mean," she smirked and winked.

The clothes hanging in the closet were a nice surprise. The silky materials, the coordinating colors, the fashionable styles. She loved pulling out the different outfits and trying them on in front of the full length mirrors on the closet doors. She was glad at one time she had taken the time to fill her wardrobe with such beautiful clothes.

Topaz, the cat, remained a mystery. He was fine with everyone else, even adored Frankie, but would have no part of Lisa. Every time she entered the room he hissed and fled. Lisa continued to care for him, but his actions were very disturbing. Beth shrugged. "He's getting kinda old, maybe he's had some kind of break down from being alone for so long. I'll take him home with me for a while. We'll see how he does in a few weeks."

Topaz went to live at Beth's house.

It was a time of adventure for Lisa. Everything was brand new and she found she felt a kinship with Frankie. Like the baby, everything she tried was the first time for her. One day she picked up the keys to her car and slipped outside. According to the wallet Beth had helped her replace, she was now a licensed driver. Would she remember how to drive?

Only one car in the parking garage could belong to her, she decided. A gorgeous little white BMW four passenger convertible. Walking to it slowly, she smiled. This was the kind of vehicle she would have chosen for herself. Pressing the alarm button on the key chain, she smiled when the car responded with flashing lights and short beep. She opened the door and nestled in under the wheel.

The seats were covered in white leather. Dark mahogany panels graced the instrument panel in front and dark blue carpet cushioned her feet. Taking a moment to familiarize herself with the car she sighed deeply. Turning the key in the ignition she heard the quiet hum of the engine as she put the car into first gear. Slowly she let the car pull forward. Turning toward the garage door she found the automatic door opener and pushed the button. Taking a deep breath, she eased out onto the quiet street.

It was like being freed from a cage, she decided and suddenly wanted to buy every bird in all the pet stores in town and set them free. Traffic made her a little nervous, and she had to pay close attention to where she was going, but for the most part her trip to the grocery store six blocks away was quite an adventure!

A few days later, Lisa was digging in the closet trying to find a belt to match the soft gray colored blouse and slacks she wanted to wear. Unaware there was a small box on top of the one she was pulling on, she cried out in surprise when the box toppled over and rained photographs over her. Stooping to pick them up she frowned. There was something vaguely familiar about these photos. Carrying them with her she went into the front room where Janet and the baby were playing on the floor.

"Janet, take a look at these. What is it about these photos that feels like I know this place?" she handed the pictures to Janet and slid to the floor to sit beside her.

Looking at the pictures Janet smiled, "This one was taken at that little gas station where we stopped to buy gas on our way here. You walked over to an antique store and found it closed, remember?"

Lisa took the picture back. She handed Janet another picture, a picture of a dark house…"I remember. The town was called Adams. Did we pass by this old house too?"

Nestled against a small hill and surrounded by ancient apple trees, Janet shook her head…"I don't remember seeing this house anywhere." She turned the photo over, "This picture was taken in the late sixties. The house may not be there anymore."

"That's true," Lisa admitted. "but for some reason I believe the house is still standing." Looking at the picture more closely she frowned, "It seems really familiar to me. I can almost see myself sitting on the doorstep…."

For long minutes Lisa sat staring at the picture. Finally she turned to Janet and smiled, "How about a trip tomorrow? Do you think Frankie might like to go bye-bye?"

"Are you planning on going back to Adams? That's a four hour drive! "

Lisa nodded. "You don't have to go with me if you don't want to. I just feel….like I have to go back there. I need to find this house."

"There's no way I'm going to let you go all that way by yourself," Janet said and picked up Frankie. "He loves to go for rides in Aunt Lisa's car. What time do you want to leave in the morning?"

It was a beautiful morning, warm and sunny. A light mist had fallen during the night leaving the air clean and full of surprising smells. Roses, honeysuckle, peonies, all the lovely smells of a late May morning swarmed their noses as they walked through the colorful garden outside the apartment to load up in Lisa's car.

The road was nearly empty early in the morning. The women talked little as they enjoyed just being out on this exquisite day. Frankie played quietly in the back seat, gurgling his baby language at the passing scenery. It didn't seem like four hours later when they pulled into the tiny store that marked the boundary of Adams.

Leaving the car to be gassed up, Lisa walked over to the antique store. Pushing against the door she was pleased when a cowbell rang merrily greeting all who entered. Inside the store she was greeted with dusty remains of other times. Shelves and tables were covered with treasures from times long past and not so long past. Dishes, furniture, house wares, clothes, and books were everywhere in the store. Carefully she walked among the aisles smiling at the whimsical, the eclectic, the absurd.

Behind the counter hung a curtain that obviously separated the public from the private...In a muffled voice she could hear a man's voice as he grunted and cursed under his breath. "Come....out....of....there...." she could hear.

Tapping on the counter she heard the male voice call out, "I'll be out in a minute! I....just....have....to....get....this....box....out!" Suddenly there was a loud crash followed by a string of expletives.

Wiping his hands on his pants the man walked from behind the curtain and turned his blue, blue eyes toward Lisa. All she saw was his dark hair and those hypnotic eyes before the room spun into a dark void.

She was aware of Janet's soft voice and touch as her senses came back to her. Kneeling on the floor beside her the young companion's worried face came into focus as Lisa's eyes began to work again. "What happened Lisa?"

"I don't know how, but....I saw Louis here. It shocked me."

"Actually you saw me," a voice said behind her. "Don't be frightened Lisa, it's me, Luke. I'm Louis' brother. Don't you remember? I'm his identical twin?"

Turning slowly she faced the man that had been behind the counter and expected to gulp with fear. Other than the initial shock, Luke didn't affect her as Louis had. She blinked a few times and looked at him closely. Even if they were identical twins, there were some slight differences. Even the short times she had been face to face with Louis she could see differences around his mouth and eyes. But more than anything, Luke didn't have the paralyzing fear effect that Louis had on her.

Holding out his hand he helped Lisa to her feet. "Perhaps you'd better have a seat for a few minutes...." he led her to a chair. "Would you like a cup of tea?"

"If it's no trouble, yes please." Lisa settled onto the chair and smiled a weak smile at Luke.

"Mom always kept a pot of water on for tea. After she died I just kept up the habit. I'll just be a moment."

Janet looked at Lisa closely then turned her attention to her son. He was rubbing his eyes and burying his face in her neck. "If you think you're all right, I'm going to take Frankie back to the car and put him down for a nap."

Lisa nodded as the young woman walked out of the store.

Luke returned in a few minutes with the tea and took a seat across from her. Staring at him she stirred her tea waiting for it to cool.

"Your friend told me you've had some kind of accident and are suffering from amnesia? How did you find your way back here?" Luke offered her some sugar but she refused.

"I found some pictures that appear to have been taken around her," Lisa said. "I came back here hoping something would jog loose my memory...There's one picture in particular, of a dark three story house, that feels familiar to me." She pulled the picture from her purse and handed it to Luke.

"It should feel familiar to you Lisa, that's where you lived for almost eighteen years. After your parents died you didn't want the house so it was sold....but that was a long time ago. The house still sits where it's always been, about six miles outside of town. I think it's empty now. The older couple that bought it have gone back east." Reaching under the glass counter he pulled out a pencil and paper. "Here, I'll draw you a map to show you how to get there...."

The winding driveway leading up the short hill even felt familiar to her as she pulled her car up to the door. Stepping out of the car she stood staring at the front of the old house. The weathered shingles, the darkened roof, the dusty window glass. She could almost feel the memories around her. Climbing the stairs she found a "FOR RENT/ LEASE/SALE" sign on the front window and pulled out a pen and paper from her purse. Quickly she jotted down the numbers.

She wandered around the property for about thirty minutes before she returned to her car. Behind the house was a huge old barn, its weathered sides shimmering gray in the afternoon sun. On the north side of the house was an apple orchard, now overgrown with briars and brush, nearly half of the trees were dead. At the end of the driveway a dark and broken tree made her frown as she drove by it.

It was a silent trip home to Vancouver. Lisa was too wound up in the sights of the house to be much company. Janet looked over at her new friend several times but didn 't intrude on her thoughts. A tired Frankie was quickly put to bed then Janet fixed a simple meal for them. Lisa paced the front room hardly seeing the view out the front window. Below her the spectacular sights of sunset over the Columbia River didn't catch her attention.

The numbers on the FOR RENT sign sat on the table next to the phone. Lisa tried one and found it to be to a local realtor, property management firm. The person she talked to could give her little information than the owner really wanted to sell but was willing to rent or lease to a potential buyer. The other number she'd tried to call several times but was unable to get an answer on the other end. She wanted more information about the place, but she wasn't sure why.

She even called Luke a few times to ask him questions. He didn't seem to mind answering them, no matter how strange the questions sounded.

"You have no brothers or sisters," he told her during one such call. "Your mother and father were killed about nine years ago. Toward the end of your senior year you got involved with a....guy at school and, well, everyone said you must have been pregnant to leave the way you did. The guy stayed here, for a while, then he disappeared after graduation. No one has heard from him since. And no one ever really knew what happened to the child.

"Your parents were killed in an automobile accident, a really sad time for everyone...Your parents were well liked. Your dad was a local businessman and your mom was a teacher. They aren't buried here, though. Someplace in Vancouver, I think."

Lisa thanked him for the information and hung up. Had she had a baby? That would have been almost twenty years ago now. Where could that person be? Was it a boy or a girl? She strained her mind thinking, but nothing. Still nothing.

It took her three days to make up her mind. She talked to Janet about it first, explaining how important it was to her to return to the house. "If I can ever get a hold of the owners!"

That evening marked the tenth time she'd tried the number. Finally, after the tenth ring an older man answered the phone. Quickly she asked about renting the house.

"Oh yes, yes, it's still for rent, but why didn't you call the realtor's office? They're the ones handling the lease...." he went on to tell her the monthly rate and a little about the place. " Mother and I often thought the place would make a perfect bed and breakfast inn, but we didn't have the energy to start one. We really would like to have a permanent person there, keeps vandals away and during the winter it keeps the pipes from freezing. We thought we had it sold a while back. A young fella wanted to bring his bride to live there but he never closed on the property. Since then we've decided to try to lease the place first, let people try it out, as it were. It's not a bad place, really. Just kind of isolated and many young people now days can't handle that. We've done a lot to fix it up. Just before mother and I left to come back east, we had a new boiler heating system installed and had the house insulated. Helps to keep the place nice and toasty in winter and cooler in summer.

After several minutes they came to a sort of agreement. Lisa would rent the house through the summer and if she liked it she would sign a year's lease with an option to buy. The owner, Mr. Thompson would contact the realtor's office and have the agreement drawn up. She could pick up the keys, sign the lease, and leave the rent check there. Thanking him she hung up.

Beth was not that easy to convince, "Why would anyone with such a beautiful apartment, wish to leave to live in such a remote area? You'll be miles away from the things you love; the theater, the night life, everything."

Lisa raised her eyebrows. Love? How would she know if she loved anything? She had no memories of the theater, the night life, or anything! All she knew was she needed to get back to Adams. Across the miles the house pulled at her, called to her. Surely returning to her roots would give her life back to her.

Chapter Four

Lisa called a mover to haul the boxes of things she wanted to take with her. Since the house in Adam was fully furnished, most of what she was taking were clothing and just a few special items from her apartment.

Excitedly she talked about the move with Janet but was surprised the young woman seemed less enthusiastic than was expected. Even when Lisa pointed out Frankie would be able to spend time outside in the fresh air and sunshine, Janet just nodded solemnly...

"I would never leave you alone, for any reason," Janet said finally..."You have been wonderful to Frankie and me, and I don't want to sound ungrateful, but....well....I'm not too excited about moving back to Idaho. My mother is probably still looking for me and Frankie."

Lisa pulled the girl to her in a gentle hug. "Oh honey, I'm sorry. I was so wound up in this move I never thought how it might affect you. If you like, you can stay here, in the apartment. I'll be ok, I can get along all right."

Janet turned teary eyes to Lisa then chuckled, "You'd starve to death in a week. There aren't any places to call for take-out in a town like Adams. No. Frankie and I will go with you and see you settled. Maybe after a little while we can look for a cook or housekeeper. Then maybe I can think about getting my own place back in the city."

The day before the move Janet took Frankie to the park for the last time. Alone in the apartment Lisa sat writing out a list of things to do. Walking into the kitchen she fixed herself a cold drink. Filling her glass with ice cubes, the phone rang... Setting the glass down on the granite counter she answered the phone.

"Hello?" she said. Moments later she heard the persistent dial tone in her ear and hung up the phone. That's odd. There was no one on the line.

Still setting where she'd left it, her glass of ice was sitting in a pool of water. Condensation off the glass had streamed to the counter top, leaving a large drippy ring around it. Most of the ice cubes in the glass were melted as well. Frowning she reached for a towel to clean up the mess. It's not that warm in here, she told herself, as she dumped the glass and fixed herself a fresh one. And the humidity isn't high in my climate controlled apartment! It was almost like the glass had been sitting for a long time but she had only been away for a moment to answer the phone.

About then the door opened and Janet and Frankie came back inside. "Did you change your mind?" Lisa asked.

Janet gave her a strange look, "We've been gone two hours, Lisa. Are you ok?"

Lisa felt a tightening in her chest but she laughed it off, "I just lost track of time." She returned to writing her list of things to do.

The drive back to Adams was filled with ambitious plans. Both women wanted to have a small garden this summer.

"Not many things, maybe some tomatoes, some lettuce, onions, that sort of things... I love fresh vegetables." Janet said quietly. "It will be fun having Frankie working alongside me in a garden."

Lisa nodded, "And I think I'd like flowers. Every kind of flower you can think of!"

They were quiet then, thinking their thoughts of fresh garden salads and colorful bouquets when Frankie fussed slightly. Rubbing his little hands through his hair he yawned noisily. Janet turned to look at her little son and smiled tenderly, " His daddy did that when he got tired," she said.

"Tell me about the baby's father," Lisa said. "You 've never told me much about him."

The young mother looked at her hands for a moment before she started. "We met at church. Mom didn't like him, of course, she never liked any of my friends…He was in town as part of a crew working on road construction. The job would last about six months, he told me. I liked him right away. He wasn't like any of the other guys at school, he was quiet and respectful. The way he talked, the way he smiled….he always made me laugh and feel good about myself. "

"We started dating, going to the movies, having supper together, that sort of thing. We went to a church dance one night and stayed late helping clean up afterwards…He had brought me a single rose and told me I was as perfect as it was." She smiled with embarrassment. "I know how corny that sounds now, but that's the kind of guy he was. I fell in love with him right then…I'd never had a boyfriend before and maybe that had something to do with it, but we ended up spending the night with one another at his motel."

"I felt so special, so loved. For the first time in my life there was someone who cared for me completely unconditionally. We were careful, used protection each time we were together. He always told me not to worry. If I got into any kind of trouble he would be there for me. His job ended about two months before graduation and he had to leave. By then he knew how awful my mom was and he wanted me to go with him. I've often wished I had. But I wanted to graduate, get my diploma. He promised he would write and call often and would be back as soon as he could."

A tear rolled down her cheek as she went on. "My mother intercepted his letters and wouldn't let me talk to him when he called. She told him all kinds of lies, told him I was seeing someone else and that I didn't want to hear from him again. Just before graduation I found out I was pregnant, but it was too late. By that time, her lies had convinced him I didn't care and he quit trying to get a hold of me."

The tears dripped from her chin as they rode silently along. Lisa felt anger rise up in her chest. What had that mother done to this girl? How could a woman treat her own flesh and blood that way? She must have said something aloud without realizing it because Janet turned to her with a quizzical look on her face.

"I thought I told you. I'm adopted. I have no idea who my real mother is. Mom said my birth mother put me up for adoption right after I was born. Mom adopted me just before I turned three."

Adams looked as sleepy as the other times they'd been there. Lisa drove up to the gas station and asked for directions to the realtor's office. Driving through the narrow streets they saw the church, the school, the post office and several small stores. One grocery store almost seemed out of place with its modern building and large parking lot. Dozens of cars lined the front of the store as people busily went about their business.

"I didn't think there were that many people in this town," Janet teased.

They quickly found the realtor's office. In minutes the key to the house was in Lisa's hand and she hurried out to the car.

"I'm too excited to do anything else right now, later we come back to town to the store and get the groceries and things we need." She started the car. "All I want to do is get to that house and get inside."

The dark tree at the end of the driveway was the first thing Lisa saw. "I wonder if Mr. Thompson would mind if I had that tree pulled out of there. I don't like it. It makes me feel creepy." Pulling up close to the house she turned to Janet and smiled, "here we go…."

"You go ahead Lisa." Janet suggested. "I'll be along in a few minutes. Frankie is still asleep but he should be waking soon."

Lisa flashed a grateful smile at the young woman. Janet nodded as she started for the stairs. She unlocked the door and watched as it slowly swung open. Breathlessly she stepped inside and looked around. A mirrored wall lay to her left with a large oak coat tree in front of it. To the side sat a small table. Ahead of her was an enormous room with a large white brick fireplace against the inside wall, built off the floor and with a brick bench in front of it. Past that was a wall of glass with French doors that led out into a solarium. Once the solarium had been filled with potted plants, flowers, possibly even birds. But now it was just a large room with low shelves along the inside walls.

To her left Lisa found herself in a formal dining room. Gleaming mahogany chairs and a table big enough for ten were protected by a dust cloth. Above it hung a glistening chandelier made of flared pink depression glass. Along each side of the room was a low sideboard and a china hutch now empty, waiting to be filled with treasures...In front of her more French doors led out onto a stone patio and beyond that an overgrown garden could be seen. The remains of a path wound through the bushes and trees, leading out toward a picturesque barn three hundred yards away.

Pushing through a swinging door she found a gourmet kitchen, big enough for a restaurant staff. Modern stainless steel gleamed at her with a six burner gas stove for cooking...She could imagine a chef with a tall white hat barking orders while a lavish meal was prepared. A small door behind the kitchen turned out to be a pantry. Another door off the kitchen led to the washer and dryer. Above the sink was a deep garden-window where Janet could grow her herbs.

"Wow!" Janet exclaimed as she walked up behind Lisa. "Look at this kitchen! We could open a restaurant with a kitchen like this."

Returning to the family room Lisa found a large archway that led into the formal living room...Another white brick fireplace and heavy overstuffed furniture filled the living room. It felt and looked too proper, too cold for her liking. Beyond the living room was a small library. Book shelves, now empty, lined the walls with a large desk sitting in the middle of the room.

She found the stairs and began to climb them. Like she was in a trance she felt herself moving through the house. Her mind was filled with a sleepy déjà vu feeling. She could feel something tugging at her mind, a memory perhaps, but nothing came to her. Whatever it was kept slipping away from her like quick silver...

There were three bedroom suites upstairs along with a large sitting room. Each room was covered with thick carpet, the walls and the comforters covering the beds were color coordinated. Janet, now close behind her, sat down in one of the rooms, with Frankie in her arms. "I think Frankie and I will take this room. There's a smaller bedroom right off this one."

Lisa nodded and headed back downstairs. A feeling of expectancy pulled her onward. She felt, rather than knew, there was a master bedroom just off the staircase. Finding the doorway she let herself in.

It was built like a small apartment. There was a day area, light and airy and filled with sunshine. Next to this room was the master bedroom. The drapes closed against the early afternoon, would fill the room with golden light. A small overstuffed chair was pulled close to the queen size bed. Lisa sat down and looked around her.

The room was done in colors of lavender, deep purple, and greens against a white background...Behind her a mirrored closet would hold her clothes. There was a bureau for her personal items. Next to the closet was a door that led into a fantastic bathroom...A garden tub surrounded by a tiled shower, a commode, two sink vanity, and a linen closet stocked with thick thirty towels. Smiling she ran her hand over the towels and looked around. She could hardly wait to fill the tub and soak in it...

A gentle tap at the door make her turn to find Janet, her eyes wide with wonder.

"This place is a mansion," she said, "I feel so out of place here!"

"Not me! This feels more like home than that stark and sterile apartment in Vancouver ever did!" Lisa smiled. "Look at this tub! We can give Frankie swimming lessons in it, it's so big. I can hardly wait to have a nice long soak in it."

Janet shook her head and chuckled, "Before you run the water we need to go back to the store and buy a few things. I've started a list. There is absolutely nothing in that gorgeous kitchen. We'll have to start from scratch stocking up on everything."

Lisa sighed, "Ok. We'll unload the car first then go back to town." Just before closing the door she gasped at the tub. I looked like it was filled with muddy water. She blinked and the image disappeared. Wordlessly she followed her young friend back out to the car.

On their way back to town Janet asked Lisa if they could have a television. "Would you think me horrible if I asked you to get us one?

I like watching a few soap operas and Frankie likes Sesame Street. Once in a while I like to watch a movie too...."

"Of course," she agreed. She assured her young companion she wanted her to be comfortable. She would see about installing a television in the kitchen and another in the family room. Since they lived so far from town she would ask about a satellite dish.

It seems hours later when they finished their grocery shopping and were back at the house quickly putting groceries away in the pantry. At least Janet was trying. Frankie was feeling overwhelmed by his new surroundings and wouldn't let his mother out of his sight. Whenever she sat him down he wailed at the top of his lungs. Finally she was forced to pick him up and try to work one handed.

"Sit down Janet and just tell me where you want things put." Lisa finally insisted. "I don't think Frankie is very happy right now and he needs you the most."

"He'll be all right," Janet assured her and nuzzled her son 's head. "He just doesn't like change. For the first few days after we moved into the apartment he wouldn't let me set him down. He'll be fine."

After finishing in the kitchen Janet carried her suitcase upstairs to settle herself and son in their rooms. Lisa could still hear Frankie protesting, but that would work itself out with time. Right now she was anxious to explore the rest of this place.

In the back porch she found a doorway leading to an unfinished basement. Turning on the light she stepped onto the stairs and looked below her. The cement floor, the huge boiler furnace, the coal bin, the place was dusty and uninviting. She shut the door behind her. Headed back upstairs she kept climbing until she was headed toward the attic. The keeper of lost treasures and memories, she'd read somewhere. Flipping on the light switch she climbed the stairs.

As expected the attic was filled with cobwebs, broken furniture, old tricycles, and a lot of boxes. Most of the boxes were covered with dust and cob webs. Before she would touch any of them she would have to clean up here. Moving to a small window she looked out across the land she had rented. Behind the house, maybe a mile away, she could see a small river meandering around through short hillsides and green fields. She shuddered and turned away.

Below her she could hear her cell phone ringing and she hurried down the stairs to answer it. Janet had beat her to it and smiled as Lisa came into the room. " Here she is Beth...."

Lisa listened a moment, "Not yet, but you have got to see this place! It's fantastic! It's like a mansion inside...."

Beth answered, "I'm looking forward to seeing it. But that' s not the reason I've called. Evidently someone broke into your apartment this morning after you left. The super at the building called me. As far as they can tell there's nothing missing. The police think whoever it was had a key....did you loose your purse again?"

Lisa assured her she still had it with her, and checked to make sure her apartment key was still on the key-ring.

"Then whoever it was must have found your old purse, the one you lost in the accident. I'll have the super change the locks and send you a new key. We'll have to call and have all of your credit cards cancelled and new ones issued." She was quiet as if she was thinking about something. Finally she said, "There was one thing really odd about the break-in. I don't know if I should tell you...."

"What was it?" Lisa demanded. "I have a right to know."

"The guy seen going into your apartment matched the description you gave of your mysterious visitor at the hospital, Louis something-or-other. One of your neighbors was just leaving her apartment and spotting him. She called the super who called the police but by the time they got there he was gone. The only evidence they found that anyone had been there was a cryptic message written across your bathroom mirror."

Lisa waited for Beth to continue. When she sensed her friend's hesitancy she asked, "What was the message?"

Beth's answer made chills run up and down her spine, "He'd written in lipstick on the mirror," Beth continued, "DON'T BE AFRAID TO REMEMBER"

Chapter Five

Over the next few days all the cob webs and dust were sought out and cleaned away. Rugs, furniture and drapes were vacuumed. The movers brought their things early that first afternoon and the two women kept busy finding places to put them. Climbing the stairs to the attic, for about the third time that day, Lisa carried an armload of empty boxes. It didn't make sense to throw them out, if they would only be staying a short time. Janet agreed storing them in the attic made sense but she was deathly afraid of spiders. The task of carrying the boxes up two flights of stairs fell to Lisa.

Tired, Lisa put the boxes down and groaned as she straightened up. She spotted an old trunk that had been pushed to one side. Next to the trunk were several old musty boxes. Inside the smaller one she could see the edges of photos peeking out. Kneeling beside the box she brushed the dust away and opened it carefully. Ancient portraits, carefully poised, some from the early 1900's, filled the box and stared back at her with empty eyes. Two family albums were inside the box. One was filled with tin-type photos, the other more modern. She carried the box downstairs to be examined later.

Finally the women were satisfied with the house. A long list of needed items had been compiled over the last several days. After going over the list Lisa decided she would have to ask someone where she should go to purchase what they needed. Leaving Janet and Frankie to rest, she pulled Frankie's car seat out of the back seat, climbed into her car and headed back to Adams. She stopped at the antique store and showed the list to Luke.

"You'll have to go to the Emporium in Jerome. It's the only store big enough to carry all that you need. It's about an hour's drive from here. Get on the highway and head due east. You can' t miss it." He handed her back the list. "Be careful though. Jerome has been plagued with a rash of car thefts lately. Be sure and lock up whenever you leave your vehicle."

It took about an hour to pull up in front of the Emporium. Locking her car carefully she walked into a large department store. In the electronics department she found the manager and explained what it was she needed. They quickly made the arrangements needed to have a satellite dish installed and the delivery of the two televisions she had picked out.

"I can expect you Tuesday then?" she said as she shook the manager's hand. No doubt she had just made his day. Commissions off this sale would net him several hundred dollars.

Nodding he assured her his team would be there by early afternoon. "If you have any problems with the installation or the equipment you can reach me at this number..." He handed her a card. Gathering the rest of her purchases she headed to her car.

It was past lunch time. Driving through the streets of Jerome she found a small family operated restaurant on the outskirts of town. Luke had told her it was a good place to eat. She turned off the ignition and straightened her clothes. Later she would insist she had locked her car doors, but she was never totally sure.

Once inside the restaurant she found a seat and waited while the waitress brought her a menu and water. After a few minutes she ordered a turkey and Swiss on whole wheat bread with coleslaw and iced-tea. The service was good, the food was excellent, and Lisa found herself relaxing over a leisurely meal. Finishing her iced-tea she stood and walked to the counter. After paying the check she walked outside...

It had been dim inside and she blinked several times before she could see properly. At first she thought her eyes were playing tricks on her. Suddenly she realized her car was gone!

It had been stolen!

Stunned it took several moments for the reality to set in. Shaking with rage she turned back toward the restaurant.

Anxiously she told the hostess what had happened and was given a phone to call the police…As she sat trembling, waiting for them to arrive she heard someone calling her name.

"Lisa? Is everything all right?"

Looking up she saw those blue eyes that always gave her a jolt, "Luke! What are you doing here? Why didn't you tell me you were coming to Jerome? NO! Everything is not all right. Would you believe someone has stolen my car!"

Before he could answer the police pulled up in front of the restaurant and Lisa met them outside to give them her statement. Giving the police a description of her car and the license plate number took several minutes. She was upset and angry by the time the police had all the information they needed.

"Great," she complained to Luke, "now how am I going to get home?"

"I'll be glad to drive you," he offered. "I'm ready to leave right now."

Gathering up her things she followed him outside to a four-wheel drive pick-up. Even though the police had assured her they would probably find her vehicle within twenty-four hours, she knew the items she'd purchased would not be in the car. And, she knew, the car could easily have been stripped, or worse. Too angry to talk she sat staring out of the window of the pick-up as they headed back to Adams.

About a mile from Adams she looked over at her driver and smiled. "I guess I'm being rude. I haven't thanked you for coming to my rescue…"

He nodded and smiled. There seemed to be something different about him today, but Lisa couldn 't quite figure out what it was. When he turned to talk to her a few minutes later she felt that strange jolt again.

"I've been wanting to talk to you Lisa, for some time now. It was lucky I ran into you in Jerome. What were you doing there today?" his voice was unnaturally quiet, almost apologetic.

"What do you mean? I asked you where to go to buy the electronic equipment I needed and you sent me to Jerome." She was beginning to feel uneasy.

Pulling up across the road from the antique store he turned to look at her, "You 've always had a problem telling us apart Lisa. I'm not Luke. I'm Louis."

Instantly her skin felt alive with chills running up and down her spine. Breathlessly she opened the truck door and practically fell out of the high riding four wheel drive…Backing away from the pick-up she ran across the road as the truck disappeared in a cloud of dust.

Stumbling into the antique store she found Luke behind the counter. He turned to her with the same face, same eyes, but not the overwhelming terror that she felt when she was around his brother.

"Lisa? What's wrong? You look like you've just seen a ghost!" He took her arm and led her to a chair.

"Louis! I just saw Louis," she whispered. "Why does he frighten me so?"

A cloud of anger crossed Luke's face. An ugly sneer pulled at his mouth and his eyes blazed. "That coward. Why in the hell didn't he come in and say hello to his brother? That bastard! It's just like him to sneak into and out of town without facing me."

Finally Lisa quite shaking. After a few minutes she explained to Luke about her car. "Is there any place around here that rents cars?"

He suggested a local gas station. "Jim doesn't really rent cars but he has a loaner he might be able to let you use for a few days." He gave her the phone number to call.

After talking with the mechanic she found out the car wasn't available until the next morning. "Could you give me a ride home?" she asked Luke.

"Sure. In a few minutes. Mrs. Peterson is suppose to be coming in to pick up a dish she ordered. She should be here any minute," he poured her a cup of tea and patted her arm. "As soon as she leaves, I'll be glad to take you home."

Ten minutes later Mrs. Peterson came to the store. She was a flamboyant lady in her late seventies that still insisted on doing things her own way. She was dressed in layers of scarves, jewelry, and a large brimmed hat. At her side she carried a huge handbag that she used as a weapon if she got upset enough. She drove her 1970 Cadillac all over the country and everyone that saw her coming gave her a wide berth. She had caused more fender benders than anyone else in the community, Jim at the gas station had told Lisa one day when she was filling up with gas. " Never been in an accident her own self, though. She just causes them."

Flaunting her soft flesh and too many pounds into the store Mrs. Peterson walked up to the counter and nodded curtly at Lisa. "Miss Miller, how are you this afternoon ?"

"Lisa had her car stolen in Jerome today," Luke offered and laid out a snowy white towel on the glass counter top.

"My dear, how horrible! Blasted little heathens in that town. Isn't safe for a lady to go anywhere these days alone." She nodded sympathetically at Lisa then turned to Luke, "Well, Luke, where's my amethyst bowl?"

Carefully Luke pulled a dark amethyst bowl from below the counter and sat it on the towel...Mrs. Peterson eyed the bowl carefully.

"This is beautiful Luke. It certainly is what I wanted. How much do you want for it?" She stared at the bowl, transfixed.

"We agreed on fifty-five dollars, remember?" Luke looked over at Lisa and winked.

"Fifty-five dollars! Luke Sammons that's robbery. You know as well as I do I can buy this same bowl in Jerome for thirty. I won't pay that much." She picked up her large bag and started walking toward the door...As she reached for the doorknob Luke picked up the bowl and in a slightly loud voice said, "Well I guess I'll have to call Mrs.

Vanly. She mentioned an interest in this bowl the day it came in and she saw me unpacking it."

Mrs. Peterson stopped in her tracks and stood at the door for several moments. Turning toward Luke she mustered her dignity and stormed back to the counter. Opening her massive purse she pulled out fifty-five dollars and threw it on the counter. Picking up the bowl she turned and left the store.

Lisa felt uncomfortable watching this display. She'd noticed how shabby Mrs. Peterson's shoes were and the car still outside the door was dented on one side and made a loud squealing noise when the wheel was turned. Like many people living in this area, Mrs. Peterson was no doubt living on her retirement checks.

Luke looked very smug as he locked up the store and led Lisa around back to his Bronco..."Do you need anything from town before I take you home?" She shook her head.

Luke chatted cheerfully as they traveled toward Lisa's house. "It was pure luck I stumbled on that bowl in Jerome. I really picked it up for little of nothing....at a garage sale of all things. Mrs. Peterson doesn't know it has a tiny nick on the bottom. I would have been willing to go forty on that bowl if she'd wanted to barter. She's so afraid old lady Vanly will get something she doesn't have, she doesn't stop to think," he chuckled. "Serves her right, the old battleaxe."

Minutes later they pulled into the driveway of the house. Luke declined an invitation for a cold drink and waved good-bye as he pulled away. Opening the front door, Lisa let herself in.

In the middle of the floor Janet sat crying. In her arms she held Frankie tightly.

"Honey! What's wrong?" Lisa asked and sat down next to her friend.

"Beth called on your cell phone a little bit ago," Janet was finally able to sob. "She said the Idaho sheriff's department had contacted her about the baby seat she purchased. They were looking for me...." she started sobbing again. "I knew they'd track me down. Beth said she told them the chair was a gift for her niece but she's not sure they bought her story."

Lisa pulled the trembling girl to her. "It'll be all right honey." For long minutes she held Janet and rocked her gently. Finally she pushed the young mother gently away from her and looked into her tear stained face. "You know, I've been thinking about your situation for some time. I think we may be going at this all wrong. We need to contact a lawyer and get you declared Frankie's legal guardian."

Picking up her cell phone she quickly dialed Beth's number. After a few minutes Beth gave her the information she needed. Making another quick call she made an appointment with a lawyer for that Friday. His offices were located in Portland, Oregon, across the river from her apartment.

"We'll head back to Vancouver tomorrow. That'll put us into town two days before the appointment. We can rest up and be ready to talk to the lawyer on Friday morning. Afterward we can head back here in the afternoon." Giving Janet another quick squeeze she smiled, "I ordered the televisions and satellite dish. They'll be delivered next Tuesday. Unfortunately I also had my car stolen…." she told her the details. "But I've rented a car from Jim and it should be here some time tomorrow. As soon as the car shows up, we'll take off."

Frankie was now asleep. Janet picked him up to carry him upstairs. A few minutes later Lisa tapped at her door and found the mother watching her baby sleep.

When Lisa entered the room, Janet looked up at her and smiled. "He's such a little angel. I can't stand the thought I might lose him. Not now. "

"That isn't going to happen Janet. I'm sure we can straighten out this mess once we talk with the lawyer." Lisa stood up. " I just came up here to tell you Jim called. He'll bring the car by first thing in the morning. We can leave as soon as it gets here."

Janet smiled through tear swollen eyes. "I don't know how I will ever be able to thank you for all you've done."

"Fate has a way of making things happen," Lisa assured her friend. "You don't know how much I appreciate what you've done for me. You've completely turned your life upside down to help me. I 'm the one that's grateful"

Chapter Six

A small compact was delivered to her doorstep the next morning. No air-conditioning, a cramped back seat and a radio that didn't work. "Sorry," the service station owner, Jim, apologized as Lisa looked over the tiny car, "It's the only vehicle I have to loan out. It runs real good though. I'm sure the police in Jerome will find your car soon, maybe you should wait…."

Shaking her head she turned to him and smiled, "Can't do that Jim. I have to get back to Vancouver for a few days. I'll be back by Friday afternoon, or Saturday morning at the latest. I'm going to leave my cell-phone number with you. If you hear anything about my car, can you give me a call ? I left your number with the Jerome police. They told me the cars they recover are often in need of repair and cleaning. You know, the kids get drunk, go for a joy ride, upchuck inside them. That sort of thing. If the police find my car can you have it towed to your station and have it cleaned and repaired?"

Jim nodded solemnly, "If that's what you want ma'am."

Frankie didn't like the tiny car. He began to fuss as soon as Janet buckled him into the seat. Janet kept apologizing to Lisa for her son's behavior. "I wish we could explain to him we're doing this for him."

Without air-conditioning they had to keep the windows down. The breeze blowing in Frankie 's face made him wail. But with the windows up it soon became unbearably hot. It was a long trip back to Vancouver.

Beth had left the new key with the security guard. He smiled and waved at the women as they made their way back to the apartment. "We had the mirror and windows cleaned while you were gone!" he called to them.

Frankie settled down as soon as they got inside. This was home to him and it made Lisa smile to see the little guy so happy again. It had been a rough couple of days for him. Picking him up he smiled at her and hugged her. Slobbery baby kisses coated her cheeks and she loved every minute of it.

Putting the baby back on the floor she walked over to the window and looked at the panoramic view below her. It did nothing for her. Although she'd been in the house in Adams only a few days, it felt more like home all ready. She hoped they'd be able to return to it in just a short time.

The appointment with the lawyer was both disheartening and encouraging. He told them right away that Janet shouldn't have taken the baby from her mother's house, especially if her mother was really the legal guardian. "Did you sign any legal papers stating you were giving guardianship of your child to your mother ?"

Janet shook her head, "The only thing I signed was a handwritten agreement stating that I would work and support all of us."

The lawyer nodded. "Hmm. I'll check the Lewiston county courthouse and see if that document was filed. Chances are it was not. In the meantime I'll start working on a petition that asks you be declared his guardian….things would have been easier if you had been beaten by your mom or if she was abusing the child, but you have a very good chance of clearing this up without too much difficulty. It would also be easier if you were married and living in your own place, but the court doesn't always take that into account any more. Do you think your mother will contest this action?"

Janet dropped her head, "I'm sure she will. She's just that way."

Lisa tried to cheer up her friend after the lawyer's appointment but little she said seemed to get through to the girl. She could tell Janet was terrified. Not only of losing her son, but of her adopted mother too. There was nothing she could do to give the girl courage, except to encourage her.

It was a hot day in Portland. The asphalt, the cement, the tall buildings all worked to hold in the heat. Close to ninety degrees outside the two women sought refuge in a small café not far from the lawyer's office.

Taking a seat in the air-conditioned dining room to enjoy their iced drinks they sat Frankie down between them in a booth.

"It sounds hopeful to me," Lisa said quietly as she handed Frankie a cracker. "I wish we'd thought of this right away, after you came to live with me. But the lawyer seems confident he will...." Lisa looked at Janet and was perplexed by her expression.

The color had drained from Janet's face and her eyes were round with astonishment...Following her gaze Lisa looked across the room and saw a young man standing with exactly the same expression on his face, staring back at Janet.

Slowly Janet came to her feet. The young man walked toward them, stopping a few feet away from their table. "Janet? I can't believe it's you. After all this time....you look good." He nodded at Lisa. "Hi, I'm an old friend of Janet's, Tom Cullen." Then his soft brown eyes fell on the baby standing beside Lisa. "And who is this little guy ?"

Tom looked at Frankie closely, frowned and then turned a bright red. Under his breath his asked Janet, "Is this your child?"

Janet nodded and sat down. She was trembling.

Tom again looked at the child and turned to her, "Is he mine?"

There were tears in her eyes as she again nodded. Tom didn't exactly sit in the chair across from them, it was more like he melted into it. It took him a few moments to grasp what he was told. Looking at Janet he was perplexed, then angry. "I'm sorry, but I'm a little confused. If you were pregnant with my child, why did you send me away? Your mom said you never wanted to see me again and all my letters came back."

The girl was crying softly and not able to answer his angry questions.

"She didn't answer your letters because her mother intercepted them and sent them back without Janet ever seeing them." Lisa answered softly...She handed Janet a napkin to wipe her eyes. "It was her mother that said all that stuff, not her. Janet wanted to tell you about the baby but her mother wouldn't let her."

Tom rubbed his forehead and wiped his hands across his face. He was visibly shaken by this news. "God Janet. I wish I'd known about all this. I hate the idea you had to face this by yourself." He was quiet for a moment, obviously uncomfortable. In a gentle voice he told her, "Listen, I'm suppose to be meeting someone....for lunch. Can I get your phone number and call you later?"

Lisa dug out a piece of paper and a pen and jotted down the apartment's phone number and address. "Come by this evening if you like. There' s more you need to know."

Tom frowned but took the paper and folded it carefully. "I hope you believe how sorry I am Janet. I had no idea what was going on. I'll talk to you later. "

"Come on honey, let's go home." Lisa said softly and helped Janet from the booth.

Paying their check she picked up Frankie and led Janet from the deli. Inside, through the glass, she saw a striking young woman approach Tom. She felt her heart fall as the woman kissed him affectionately and sat down at his table. Looking at Janet she was relieved to see she had not been watching. She was too upset to notice...

Muscles ached and her head felt like it was going to explode. It had been a long day. Janet was still upset, barely able to function. Lisa had been taking care of Frankie most of the day. Unused to holding him so much and picking him up as much as she had, she felt like her back and neck were ready to break. While both of them napped she decided to have a long soak in her tub.

Running the warm water she filled the tub with fragrant bath beads. As the steam filled the room she slipped into the water and sighed. Closing her eyes she allowed the heat to relax her aching body. A rolled up towel under her head made her comfortable as she lay in the fragrant suds.

She must have dozed for a few minutes or perhaps she was really asleep, but she opened her eyes to his dark hair and blue eyes gazing at her. He was sitting on the edge of the tub. This time she wasn't afraid of him. She smiled at him like she'd known him forever. He smiled back and touched her face gently. Leaning over the tub he kissed her lips.

Her eyes jerked open then. But she could still feel the warmth of his mouth on hers. Looking around the room she was relieved to see no one was in the bathroom with her and lay back again trying to quiet her thudding heart. It was only a dream she told herself. Suddenly she gasped. The steam on the glass of the mirror had revealed the remains of his cryptic message written and cleaned away days before;

DON'T BE AFRAID TO REMEMBER

* *

The guard called up from the foyer and told them they had a visitor. A Tom Cullens was calling...Should he send him up? Janet sat down hard on the couch when Lisa told her, but nodded her agreement to let him join them.

He walked hesitantly into the room and looked around. Spotting Frankie he offered him a small package. "Here you go fella. I thought you might like this."

Frankie knew a present when he saw one and began to pull the paper away from the brightly colored box. Kneeling beside the boy Tom laughed when Frankie pulled the car from the box and immediately put it in his mouth.

"He sure is a good looking little guy. What's his name?" Tom took a seat across from Lisa.

"I named him Franklyn." Lisa answered in almost a whisper. " He's twenty months old."

It was obvious Tom was doing some quick mental math. Satisfied he smiled at Janet. "My middle name is Franklyn."

"I know," she said.

"I....ah....owe you an apology Janet. I didn't mean to seem rude this morning. When I didn't hear from you and your mom said you didn't want to see me anymore, I went on with my life. About a year ago I met someone... We've been dating seriously for some time now. In fact, we' ve talked about getting married at the end of this summer."

Lisa watched Janet closely. She was proud of the way she handled the news.

"Congratulations," Janet said quietly.

Lisa waited a few minutes but neither of them said much to each other. Finally she said, "There are a few things you need to know Tom." She turned to Janet hoping the girl would speak up. When she didn't Lisa continued. "Janet's mother not only convinced you, you were not welcome, but she also forced Janet to give up the care of Frankie to her. Until a few weeks ago, Janet and her son lived with her mother but Janet was not allowed to do anything for him. Her mother was keeping her captive and forcing her to work under the threat she would have Janet proven an unfit mother."

"At about the time Frankie turned eighteen months old I entered the picture. Janet was working at a hospital where I was taken after an accident. I have amnesia and the doctors felt I needed someone to stay with me so I asked Janet if she was willing to move to Vancouver and stay with me. That's how she ended up here."

Taking a deep breath Janet explained further, "When I got ready to leave I packed a few things for Frankie and myself and ran away. Since then my mother has told the police she has legal custody of the boy and has had them looking for me. Unfortunately they may have traced me as far as to Lisa's friend, Beth. Beth bought Frankie a car seat before we left town and they traced her through the credit card slip."

"We were in town today to talk to a lawyer. He says I have a fairly good chance of proving myself to be a fit mother and have Frankie put into my custody." Frankie toddled over to his mother and showed her his car. "What a pretty car, Frankie. Can you tell the nice man, thank-you?"

"Tank-oo," Frankie cooed and sat down to play again.

Tom smiled, "He sure is a neat kid." He scratched his cheek for a moment..."How can I help? Do you need money or anything? I mean, I' m not sure what to do or what is expected of me at this point...."

Janet's eyes flashed. "I don't expect anything from you. Frankie is *my* son. It would have been wonderful if things had worked out between us, but they didn't. I don't need anyone's help now, except for Lisa's. Don't feel you are obligated in any way to do anything."

Tom's face blazed. "I'm sorry. I didn't mean to offend you. If I had known about the kid things would have been different Janet. How can you blame me for something I didn't even know existed until this morning?"

They were quiet then, for many long minutes. Lisa cleared her throat and stood, "Would either of you like something cold to drink? I think there's iced-tea and Pepsi in the refrigerator."

"Nothing for me, thanks," Tom answered sullenly.

Janet shook her head.

Lisa left the room and tried not to listen as the two began to talk again in quiet tones...She fixed herself an icy soft drink and slowly came back into the living room...It was awkward being a part of this, but she didn't want Janet to think she was deserting her. She sat down at the far end of the couch.

Nothing was really settled that night. Tom left shortly after Lisa returned from the kitchen, but he promised he would return the next day. Janet was scheduled to meet with her lawyer again, Monday afternoon. Tom insisted he be there with her. Janet insisted it wasn't necessary.

"It's necessary to me," he replied heatedly. "I'm not going to let you push me away Janet. I'm not trying to horn in on your life or

Frankie's, but I have an interest in this too. What your mom did to you was awful, but she hurt me too. Until this morning I didn't even know I was a father. But I do now and I'm not going to let you go through anymore of this alone. I wish I could do more....but like I said before....there's someone else in my life now."

As soon as the door shut behind him, Lisa turned to her young friend. "I like him Janet. He seems like a decent sort of man. And he seems genuinely concerned about you and Frankie. I honestly think he wants to help you any way he can."

Janet picked up a very sleepy Frankie and nodded at Lisa, "I guess so. I'm....going to get Frankie ready for bed." She left the room then, and Lisa didn't see her again the rest of the night. But for most of the night Lisa could hear her quiet sobs from the other end of the apartment.

Chapter Seven

Like a caged animal Lisa began to pace the front room. The longer she stayed in the apartment the more she ached to return to the house in Adams. Every day she was here, the stronger the pull to return.

Janet watched her friend and finally sat her down, "Listen Lisa. I can handle things here for a while. If you don't mind being alone in that house, that is. You can purchase some TV dinners and makings for sandwiches. If you have fresh fruit and ready to eat desserts you won't starve. By the end of the week I should have some idea what the lawyer is planning on doing. I'll let you know."

There was a definite change in Janet and Lisa like it. No longer meek and mousey the girl was ready to fight for what was rightfully hers. Something about seeing Tom had snapped her out of the "poor little me" phase she was going through. A woman now stood ready to take on whatever was necessary to carve a niche for herself and her son.

Excitedly Lisa began to make plans to return to Adams. She would leave first thing in the morning, while it was still cool outside and the traffic was light. Torn between wanting to stay longer, go to the lawyer with Janet, and return to her roots, Janet made her mind up for her.

"I need to start standing on my own two feet. How can I prove myself a fit mother and guardian if I can't fight my own battles? You need to get back to that house. It's obvious to me something is about to happen, maybe your memory is about to return. But be careful."

Janet was working in the kitchen, "Would it be all right with you if I stay here? I can start looking for a place of my own in a few days."

Lisa smiled, "Right now I'm ready to sign over the apartment to you but that's a little premature. Stay as long as you like, honey. Don't feel like you have to hurry out and find your own place. Why not ask the lawyer what he thinks. Explain to him about our arrangement. I pay you a wage for being my companion, nurse and housekeeper-cook."

The drive back to Adams was long, hot and tiring. She missed the friendly talk of Janet and the baby's silly babble. By the time she reached the antique store she was too tired to be friendly. Stopping at the service station she asked Jim if he'd heard anything about her car.

"Didn't the police call you?" he asked. "I' m towing your car back here tomorrow. They found it this morning, outside Jerome in a ditch. I guess one fender is crumpled and the inside has been trashed. Better call your insurance adjuster, you're gonna have to send in a claim."

Just what I needed to hear, Lisa told herself as she climbed back into the tiny compact...Pulling into the store's parking lot she hurried about finding the items Janet had suggested. TV dinners, sandwich makings, bottled drinks, snacks, fruit...She filled her cart and checked out.

It was close to noon by the time she drove up the driveway of her house. The sun was beating down on the countryside. An early summer heat wave, she'd heard in town. Everyone in the west was suffering from it. Opening the front door she was pleased to find the inside cool and comfortable. One thing about some older houses, they were built right and with the new insulation, the place kept out the weather!

It took several trips from the car to the front door to unload the groceries and her bags...The house sounded hollow, empty, without Janet and Frankie. Oh well, she told herself, the televisions and satellite dish would be delivered day after tomorrow...In the meantime she could do some more exploring. She hadn't been out to the barn yet.

A quick lunch of fruit and cold cuts and she felt refreshed. Wandering around the house she found a closet just off of the utility room, bare inside with only a few padded hangers. Off of the library she found a small bathroom, the toilet in dire need of a good scrubbing. In the solarium she found a small artificial waterfall, now long dry. Finally she turned to her room. She was the most familiar with this room now. Spotting the old box of pictures she sat down to look at them.

Obviously the pictures were not in any order. The album sat on top of piles of photos, rubber banded together. Had they been gathered together by someone and just thrown into this box? Taking the time to sort through the pictures, Lisa smiled when she came to several photos of an older couple holding a beautiful little blonde girl in their arms. They were standing in front of this house, smiling back at whoever took the pictures. No doubt grandma and grandpa pictures, Lisa told herself.

Dusting her hands off on her pant leg she looked around. It was going on to two in the afternoon. From her bedroom window she could see the barn inviting her to come explore. Pulling on an old pair of running shoes she let herself out of the house into the overgrown back garden.

I need to get a hold of someone to clean up this yard, she told herself as she walked along the stone path. She quickly make her way to the towering doors of the barn... To one side of the huge doors was a much smaller one, held closed by a small board nailed through the middle. Turning the crude lock she pulled the door open...

Barnyard smells never quite leave a place once they permeate the wood and floors. The barn had obviously not been used for livestock for many years, but the smell of manure lingered on. Inside the door a huge open area lay. Above her she could see dusty sunlight peeking through the cracks in the roof and the upper walls. Small open areas along the eaves allowed for air circulation and patchy sunlight in the hay loft.

Above her head, maybe fifteen feet high, a ladder stretched to the upper floor. Curious about what might be up there, she pulled herself up onto the ladder. Carefully she tested each step before she put her full weight on the wooden rung. Cautiously she stepped onto the loft boards.

One large room stretched before her. It was empty except for the scurrying of field mice as they hurried to find a hiding place. Shivers of disgust went through her as she saw a rat hurry by. Above her the ceiling was alive with fat furry bodies, writhing inside their leathery wings. Stifling a scream Lisa hurried back to the ladder. Bats. Mice. Rats. Ugh!

She shouldn 't have hurried she told herself. That was her second mistake. Her first was ever exploring a place like this alone. She knew better. Laying there on the floor the ceiling spinning above her and the pain shooting through her right ankle, she told herself again she knew better. Above her she could see the broken rung that had given way in her haste to get back to the barn floor. She was lucky she hadn't broken her leg. It was more than a ten foot drop.

Shaking her head with self disgust she looked around for something to use as a crutch. Unfortunately the barn had been thoroughly cleaned out and there was nothing usable within grasp.

It took her awhile to be able to stand. Her ankle was badly sprained from the look of the swelling and the pain it was causing her. There was no way she could put any weight on it and she knew it was too far to try to hop all the way back to the house. She'd have to crawl. The thought made her cringe but there was no other way to get back to the house. She cursed her luck for not remembering to bring her cell phone.

Angrily she scolded herself every miserable foot back. She had to stop frequently. Tipping her ankle to keep from touching the ground so she could crawl made pain shoot through it. She would crawl several yards then turn over and allow the nerves in her foot to quit screaming. Bracing herself she then returned to all fours and crawled several yards more.

It took her hours to reach the back path. In the house she could hear the shrill bell of her cell phone. Shaking her head she hoped whoever it was calling had the courtesy to call back, later. At last she was at the back door. Opening the screen and then the back door, she braced herself against the door frame to catch her breath…By the time she reached the family room she was exhausted. Covered in grass stains and dirt she slumped into a recliner. Carefully she lifted the foot rest under her throbbing ankle. Laying back she tried to relax.

Somehow over the next few hours she was able to fix herself an ice pack for her ankle and find some aspirin. Figuring it would be easier to just go to her room she managed to sponge off most of the dirt, change her clothes and hopped back to her bed. Her cell phone began to ring.

"Hi Lisa, it's Janet!" her young friend's voice sounded better, more relaxed. "How was your trip back to Adams?"

For a moment Lisa almost told her friend about her accident but decided not to. The young mother had enough to worry about right now. Instead she told her how hot it was here, and how much she missed the two of them. She told her about exploring the barn. Moving her foot to try to get more comfortable she gasped with pain.

"Are you all right?" Janet's voice was filled with concern…

"I'm fine. I just cut my finger on a book I'm trying to read," she lied. She didn't want Janet trying to figure out some way to hurry back to care for her klutzy friend.

After a few minutes Janet said good-bye and hung up. Laying back against her pillows Lisa caught her breath. Damn. This wasn't going to be as easy as she thought. Maybe she should call someone for help.

Most of the evening she went from being desperate to get some help, to being fiercely independent. By the time the phone rang again at 8:30 she had made up her mind she was going to do this on her own. It would be nice if she had a pair of crutches, but she would manage without them somehow. About then her phone rang again.

Luke's deep male voice answered her hello, "Hey, how come you didn't stop by when you got into town? I've missed you."

Lisa sighed, "I'm sorry. It was hot, I was tired and I needed to buy some easy to prepare groceries."

"Where's your little friend? Didn't she come back with you ?"

Briefly Lisa explained to him about Janet staying in her apartment, leaving out the parts of the lawyer and Tom.

For several minutes they talked back and forth. Finally Luke asked what she was doing tomorrow... When she asked why he answered, "I'm planning a picnic. There 's a lovely waterfall above the old farmhouse where you're living and I thought we might hike back there tomorrow...."

She couldn 't help but laugh at his timing. "I wasn't going to say anything to anyone, but I....ah....fell today and sprained my ankle."

Luke's voice suddenly took on a serious note, "How badly are you hurt?"

"My ankle resembles a small melon, and it hurts like hell, but I think I'll be all right." She tried to make light of it, laugh it off, but he wouldn't hear of it.

"Have you seen a doctor?" He asked and when she said no he told her, "I'll be there in about ten minutes. I'm taking you to the hospital in Jerome. You could have a broken foot!"

It was a long uncomfortable trip to Jerome. And it was a long uncomfortable wait in the emergency room. Finally, a young doctor looked at her ankle and frowned. "You're going to have to have an x-ray, ma'am. This looks like it might be broken."

It was fractured. A brace, wrapped with an ace bandage, some muscle relaxants and pain pills and three hours later they were headed back toward Adams.

Luke said, "You shouldn't be alone tonight."

Lisa replied, "I don't really know anyone else that could stay with me...."

Luke sat quietly behind the wheel of his Bronco for a while. "I can stay with you, at least for a few days. I'm not expecting anything to come into the store and Mondays and Tuesdays the store is closed anyway. Let me stop by my place and pick up a few things...."

Lisa protested but he would not listen. "You can't be on your foot, the doctors says not to put any weight on it for at least three days. You can 't cook, you told me that yourself, which means you'll be living off of TV dinners and the like....and you'll be taking some powerful medication that could make you lightheaded. I think that means you need someone, for just a few days, to watch out for you."

No matter how much she protested, he insisted. She felt uncomfortable with the idea but didn't know how to tell him without hurting his feelings. Finally she decided she could handle it for a couple of days. While she waited for him outside his store, she tried not to let a feeling of despair overtake her.

It's probably the medication, she told herself.

He insisted on carrying her into the house. Swooping her up into his strong arms he managed the steps and the front door without any problems. Smiling, he carried her to the family room couch and set her gently down. Almost giddily he told her, "I'll run out and get my things and be right back!"

Lisa didn't like this new side to Luke. He was acting too strangely, but she settled herself into the couch determined to make the best of the next few days...And right now she was too tired to care. It was after midnight and she was exhausted...Pulling her crutches under her arms she made her way to her room.

Moments later she heard a gentle tap on her door, "Lisa? Are you all right?"

"I'm fine Luke. I'm just really tired. You can sleep in one of the rooms upstairs if you like, but I have to get some rest. We'll talk more in the morning." She watched the door, her heart pounding. What was she afraid of? She didn't know, but she wished she'd locked her bedroom door before getting into bed.

"All right. I'll see you in the morning. Sleep tight. If you need anything, just call out. I'll be sleeping on the couch in the family room." She heard his footsteps echoing away as he turned away from her door.

Slipping down into the sheets she yawned drowsily. The pain medication Luke had insisted she take, the muscle relaxant the doctor had given her, were making it impossible for her to stay awake. Waves of drowsiness washed over her. She wanted to fight the sleepiness, but didn't know why. Finally she again yawned noisily and allowed her eyelids to close. In moments she was asleep.

Unsettling dreams plagued her slumber. Several times during the night she dreamed there was a man in her room. It was dark and she was unable to see his face. Each time she startled awake only to find herself alone, but it was hard to shake the feeling of an intruder.

By morning she was still tired. Her foot throbbed and her head ached. About eight in the morning Luke tapped at her door. "Hello sleepyhead! Are you awake in there?" Turning the knob he let himself into her room. "I hope you're decent.... breakfast is now being served."

In his hands he held a tray loaded with food. Eggs, toast, bacon, juice and melon slices...The smells nearly gagged her. Groggily she looked up at him. "Thank-you but I usually don't eat such a big breakfast. The toast and juice will be fine. Why don't you eat the rest of it for me?"

His face fell in disappointment. "I cooked all this for you. I've already eaten. At least try some of it. I have a special way of preparing scrambled eggs that makes them light and fluffy. And the bacon....you gotta try it....it's crisp all the way through without being greasy or dried out."

Afraid of hurting his feelings she tried everything on the tray and ate most of it. It was good, she told him. Smiling wearily she again insisted it wasn't necessary for him to stay with her. "I really appreciate your concern and your willingness to do this, but I don't think I need an around the clock nurse. Maybe you could call me a couple of times a day to make sure I'm all right."

"Nonsense, it's a ten minute drive from town to out here. What if you needed help right away? What if you fell again?" he persisted and picked up the tray. "I'll be back in with your medication in a few minutes. In the meantime, relax, I've got everything under control."

Again she had a feeling of misgivings.

By the time he brought in her pills her whole leg was throbbing. Frowning she looked at the three pills on a small tray. "Where's the medicine bottles Luke? I like to read the directions and take my medication on my own."

"Think about it Lisa," he answered with a stern face. "This medicine is pretty powerful stuff. The doctor told you it would make you lightheaded and dizzy. If you have the bottles next to you, you might accidentally take more than you should. If I bring the medication to you, we'll know exactly how much you are taking. I had to do the same thing for mother when I took care of her. Believe me, it's safer this way."

Reluctantly she agreed. Picking up the pills she frowned, "I thought the prescriptions said to take one pain pill and one muscle relaxant every four to six hours. There 's three pills here."

"Actually the pain medication said take one *or* two tablets every four hours as needed. The muscle relaxants you take every six hours. I figured having slept the night through without medication your foot must be pretty painful by now." He sat down in the chair beside her bed, "Are you going to question everything I do Lisa? Don't you trust me?"

She felt the blood rise in her cheeks, "No....I mean of course I trust you. I do appreciate what you're doing. It's just that I'm not used to someone doing all this for me and I have to admit I'm a little bit cranky this morning."

He smiled then, a brilliant smile that lit his face. Lisa quickly downed the medication.

"Of course you're cranky. You go ahead and rest. I'll be back in to check on you in a few hours. If you need anything, holler. I' ll bring you a pitcher of water in case you get thirsty. Do you want me to help you to the bathroom before I leave?"

"That's all right. I took care of that before you came in this morning," she noted the strange look on his face. There was no way she was going to allow him to take her to the bathroom! As she nestled into her bed she told Luke, "Oh by the way, I bought a couple of TVs and a satellite dish when I went to Jerome last week. They're suppose to be delivered either today or tomorrow."

The ugly look that crossed his face, for only a split second startled her. "I'll be watching for them," he called over his shoulder and let himself out of her room.

She slept most of the morning. The strong medication sent her into a narcotic slumber that made things seem unreal to her. She was aware of Luke giving her more medication and she remembered thinking it was too soon, but she didn't argue. As she drifted back to sleep she had to admit her leg felt better.

He brought her a tray at noon and insisted she eat some of it, but the medication had taken her appetite away. Sullen and cross he pouted as he carried the tray of food away...He was back in the room a few minutes later, with more pills. Half asleep she took them, then looked over at the clock. It was hard to see the face, her eyes not wanting to focus, but she thought it said twelve-fifteen. Groggily she lay back against the pillows and fell back to sleep.

It seemed only minutes later Luke was back with another pill. She opened her mouth and took it obediently. Laying on her side she looked at the clock and tried to get her eyes to focus. It said two-thirty!

That can't be right, she told herself. Maybe the power went off and my clock wasn't reading the right time. But she knew that wasn't it either...She didn't want to believe what else it could be.

Why would Luke overdose her on her medication this way? It was dangerous to give someone too much of a narcotic drug. They could quit breathing. She remembered what he had said earlier, about his mother, and having to watch the medicine she was taking...With that kind of experience behind him he knew better than to give too much of the pain pills to anyone.

It was hard to stay awake, but she forced herself to. She got up, locked herself in the bathroom and took a cold shower. Now chilled, but more alert, she limped out to the chairs in her day area and propped her foot up on an ottoman. She needed something to concentrate on, something that would help her stay alert. She found a deck of cards and started playing solitaire. Several times over the next hour she nodded off, but woke with a start after only a few minutes.

It was just four o'clock when Luke came to her door again. Shocked at finding her up, he insisted she return to bed at once.

Steeling herself she turned blazing eyes on him, "Luke! Stop this! I am not an invalid. I want to stay up, so I will. I appreciate what you've been doing for me, but it's time for you to go home!" Before he could protest she turned to him and in a very firm voice said, "I insist!"

Sighing heavily he sat down in a chair close by, "I'm sorry Lisa. I guess I really do come on too strong at times. I didn't mean to. No more forcing you to eat, or to take your medicine, or anything. I'll fix you a supper tray, then I'll leave. Would you like some tea before I go?"

"That would be nice. Thanks." She smiled at him. Maybe she' d been a little paranoid, but she would rest easier knowing he wasn't in the house.

It took only a few minutes for him to return with a pot of steaming tea. He sat it and a cup next to her.

"My own secret recipe," he told her as he poured her a cup. "It's raspberry flavored black tea, with a hint of lemon and honey. I hope you like it."

Lisa sipped the tea and smiled, it was delicious.

"Good. I'll bring you a supper tray in just a few minutes, then I'll let myself out." he turned and left the room.

The tea was very good, she had to admit. And it soothed her jangled nerves. There was a bit of a funny aftertaste to it but she thought it was from the raspberry and fruit flavors. She finished the first cup and poured herself another.

She was starting to relax. Yawning she laid out another game of solitaire. She hated how pain pills always left her feeling hung over. She was still drowsy and found herself fighting off sleep again. Finishing the second cup of tea didn' t do much to help either. Finally she decided not to fight it, Luke was leaving after all, she hobbled over to her bed.

Sleep overtook her immediately. It was a deep sleep too. Even at a subconscious level she knew this sleep wasn't right. She tried to pull herself up, but couldn 't do it.

Time had no meaning for her. She drifted in and out of the deep sleep. At one point she opened her eyes and dreamed Luke was standing over her, a queer look on his face. Unable to talk or reason, she drifted off again.

She thought someone was climbing into bed with her.... or was she dreaming? His body was warm and hard against her in her snowy sheets and her unreal world. Sighing she tried to tell him not to touch her there and tried to push his mouth away but she had no strength. His hands gripped her breasts and she cried out softly, but there was no will to fight, no strength of morals to reinforce her.

Deep in her mind she knew she was about to be raped and all of her moral attitudes was fighting against the intruder, but again the trance she drifted in took away her determination. She felt his hands all over her, knew what his intentions were but was unable to defend herself.

Just at the moment he was ready to thrust himself upon her, she heard a startled gasp from him and felt him jerked away. In the darkened room she could make out the fuzzy form of two men. One naked, the other as tall and powerful as the other, but dressed in dark clothing. Through hazy eyes she saw them struggling. Her attacker was pushed hard, against the table where the tea pot sat. She heard the pot fall and shatter. Her rescuer, punched and slapped the nude intruder, until whimpering, he fled the room.

Blue eyes filled with anger and concern looked down on her. Through the haze she heard him ask if she was all right, but she didn't have the strength to answer him. Was it Luke that had come to her rescue? Who was the other man? She couldn 't tell but whoever her rescuer was now took her in his arms and set her upright on her painful ankle. He was making her walk, trying to sober her up.

Strong black coffee was held to her lips and although it gagged her to drink it, drink it she did. Through still unfocusing eyes she saw his blue eyes, still filled with concern look deep into hers. "Lisa, my beloved Lisa, you must remember...Everything depends on you remembering. Don't be afraid. I' ll be there with you."

* *

Was it all a dream? She asked herself that as she slowly sat up on her bed. It was early morning now, the birds sang merrily outside her window. She was dressed, in a sweat suit, and beside her bed was a half empty cup of strong coffee. Yawning she slipped her feet to the side of the bed. Her head was pounding and she put her hand up to it. Was Luke still here? She called his name softly but heard only the gentle creaking of the house as it warmed by the sun.

Looking around the room she saw no sign of a struggle. The furniture was upright, there was no spot where tea could have been spilled. Was it all a dream?

Limping into the bathroom she looked around the massive room and frowned. She needed aspirin desperately. On the floor was her nightgown. She never left her lingerie laying around like that. Picking it up she put it in the hamper. Suddenly she froze. On the mirror in front of her, in bright red lipstick, was the message:

DON'T BE AFRAID TO REMEMBER! I'LL BE THERE WITH YOU!

Chapter Eight

It was hard getting to the door but the insistent knocking at the front was compelling...Finally she made her way to the entry and opened the door. On the front step stood a distinguished looking police officer. Beside him was a well dressed couple in their mid-fifties.

"Ms. Miller? I'm officer Bryant. This is Mr. and Mrs. Charles Lamont...They're the parents of one of the boys implicated in the theft of your car. They'd like to talk to you for a few minutes. May we come in?" The officer had slowly been easing his way forward until he stood in the doorway...

Lisa nodded and opened the door wide. The trio walked into her family room and stood waiting while she hobbled into the room behind them. "Please take a seat...I apologize for making you wait, as you can see I injured my foot a few days ago."

Mrs. Lamont was dressed in a stylish form fitting suit. Her hair and make-up were salon perfect. She sniffed haughtily, smiled weakly and took a seat on the edge of one of the chairs. Her husband stood above the group looking around the room. He wasn't very tall, but was dressed in slacks and a polo shirt. His hands fascinated Lisa. The nails were manicured and polished. He turned to the mantle and picked up a picture of Janet and Frankie, frowned and returned the picture to the mantle.

The officer was the first to speak. "Ms. Miller, the Jerome police have arrested Kyle Lamont in connection with the theft of your car. Mr. and Mrs. Lamont are here to make an offer to you."

Mr. Lamont cleared his throat, "Ms. Miller we are prepared to restore your car to its pre-damaged condition and offer you a sizeable settlement for the suffering you have experienced. We will do this if you will agree to drop the charges against our son, and settle out of court." Mr. Lamont handed a document to Officer Bryant. "All you have to do is sign this agreement and we will forward whatever amount you deem necessary to put this ordeal behind you."

"Kyle is a very troubled young man," his mother said stiffly. "He has been disillusioned by his peers and has a hard time dealing with the pressures of his group of friends. We have had him in therapy for several years, which seems to be benefiting him. However, if he is convicted of this crime, he will most likely, have to go to jail....his counselor has advised us that will scar him for life....he may never get over it."

"If it's his first time, I'm sure the judge will take the extenuating circumstances into consideration." Lisa offered.

"Well....this isn't the first time Kyle has been in trouble with the law...." Officer Bryant said but stopped at the glare he received from Mr. Lamont. Lisa didn't miss the looks exchanged between the two men.

Awkwardly she stood and looked down on the trio in her family room. She was feeling more than just a little angry. "I'm sorry. I have decided to let the insurance company handle this. If you have a problem with their decision then I suggest you contact my insurance adjustor in Vancouver. His name is Gerald Barns...I can get you his number if you like...."

The Lamonts stood, their faces blazing. Officer Bryant folded the paper and slid it into his pocket. "I see. In that case Ms. Miller, I guess we have no further business here. We can let ourselves out."

The nerve of some people! Lisa thought as she watched the limousine drive away. Just because they have money they expected me to sign the problem away. There is nothing those folks could do that would make me feel like I was going to let their little Kyle off the hook.

Another knock at the door and she hobbled back to the entry. Thinking the Lamonts had returned to increase their offer she was ready to do battle. She opened the door to find two workmen dressed in coveralls.

"'Lo ma'am. We're here from the Emporium," one man offered her an ID badge. "We're here to install your satellite dish and your televisions."

She smiled warmly at the men and stepped back from the door. Three hours later she was set up with all the channels she would ever want to watch. Instead of installing the smaller TV in the kitchen, she had it installed in her bedroom suite. Later she would order another small TV to be placed in Janet's room.

Jim called shortly after that. He had her car at the station. Would she care to look at it before he started work on it? She said she wanted to see it. She'd be there as quickly as she could.

The drive to town was difficult. She had to use her left foot for the gas and the brake, but she took it easy and arrived without mishap. She went directly to the service station and pulled up outside the bay door. Hobbling inside on her crutches she could see the back of her little white BMW convertible. From where she stood it didn't look too bad. But moving to the side of the car, she was shocked! Along the passenger's side and across the front of the vehicle the paint had been scraped away with dents and creases. The hood of her car was creased across the middle and folded in half. Inside she could see the radio/CD player, and speakers had been yanked out. The convertible's top had been slashed and hung in ugly tears. The back seat was covered with an oily stain and the floor was littered with beer cans. Her car had been thoroughly trashed. Could it be put back together again?

Jim came into the bay, wiping his hands on a red rag. Pushing his stained hat back from his black hair he scratched his cheek. "Might be better if'n you traded this little beauty off and just got yer self a new one. The insurance company will mos' likely total it. This is gonna take some doin' to get her fixed up."

Lisa turned to him and managed a weak smile. "Do the best you can Jim. My insurance man has told me they can ship all the parts you need directly to you," she handed him a slip of paper with the name and phone number of the adjuster..."Give him a call. This little car means a lot to me."

Driving slowly past the antique store she was surprised to see the sign CLOSED INDEFINITELY on the door. Not much was clear about the night of her almost rape, but she had wanted to talk to Luke about it. The more she thought about it, the more she was convinced he had been the one that saved her. The message on the mirror had her stumped, though. It didn't make any sense.

She didn 't understand the medication thing either. The day after Luke left she searched the kitchen and dining room looking for her prescription bottles but they were gone. Why would he have taken them?

Pulling into the grocery store parking lot she managed to get inside the store and grabbed a shopping cart. Leaning against the cart she slowly made her way through the aisles of the store. She needed more fresh fruit and wanted some soup and crackers...Stopping in front of the rows and rows of canned soups she stood there trying to decide which ones she wanted. On the other side of the aisle she could hear Mrs. Peterson talking with someone....

"....his face covered with bruises" "....could hardly walk....." "I didn't feel sorry for him though, always thought he was some kind of...." "....took off from town and left his store...." "....did this once before....years ago got into it with his brother...." "beat the hell out of him."

Lisa tried not to listen to the gossip in the other aisle but her skin was crawling. Was it Luke they were talking about? Hurrying around to the other side she was disappointed both women were gone. Trembling she put her hand to her head. She felt sick, nauseous. What had happened? Had it been Luke that attacked her?

Finishing her shopping she hurried as fast as she could from the store.

Back at the farmhouse she just made it back inside and was settling into her room to watch TV when her cell phone rang. Picking it up she heard the merry voice of her agent, "Hi kiddo! How ya doing? Are you ready to give up this nonsense and return to your apartment?"

It was good to hear her voice. Lisa missed her friend and they spent several minutes just chatting on the phone. Finally Lisa talked Beth into coming for a visit that weekend. Agreeing, Beth said good-bye and started to hang up. "Oh! I almost forgot why I called you, scatter brain that I am. I was contacted by the Idaho police again. They're getting kind of insistent. I called my lawyer to ask his advice. He's told me if they call back I'd better 'fess up. If not they can hold me as an accomplice to kidnapping. Sorry, I thought I should let you know. In the meantime, I'm letting my answering machine screen my calls. If I don't talk to them, I won't have to tell them anything."

Lisa thanked Beth and hung up. She had better let Janet know what was going on. Dialing the apartment she got the answering machine. No doubt Janet and the boy were out shopping or at the park. She left a message on the machine to call her back right away.

Sitting on her couch, she switched on the TV. An old movie flashed onto the screen and she nestled back in the cushions to watch it. It was an old John Wayne, Maureen O'Hara film, *The Quiet Man*. It was a movie she'd seen several times and soon she dozed off.

She knew she was dreaming. A stormy night was all around her. She was in a vehicle, headed through pounding rain, alongside a rushing, flooded river. An unknown man was at the wheel. They were arguing. Every few minutes the faceless driver leaned over and yelled something at her. She felt angry, confused and a little afraid.

The truck began to skid. The driver tried to stop, slammed on the brakes, the truck started spinning out of control....suddenly a huge dark tree, old and knarled, was in front of them. Then there was darkness and a feeling of suffocating.

She woke up coughing and fighting to breath. Falling off the couch she went to all fours before she was able to pull the air back into her aching lungs. Shaken she sat back against the couch, on the floor, until her breathing eased and she quit trembling...Trying to stand she stepped on her fractured ankle wrong and felt a crunching pain shoot through it. Immediately the foot began to throb again.

"Damn!" Lisa muttered and fell back against her couch. She pulled her aching foot up beside her and waited to see if the throbbing would ease. It didn 't. Afraid she might have re-fractured the foot she reached for the phone...There was no way she could travel clear to Jerome. Dialing Jim's number at the station she waited impatiently until he answered the phone.

"Jim? This is Lisa Miller. Is there a doctor in Adams?"

"Yes'm there is. Doc Mary is in town, right across from the post office...She's semi-retired but takes emergency cases. She listed under Mary Scope, MD."

The voice that answered sounded sweet, concerned and very professional. "I only see emergency patients now...." she explained. "What is the problem?"

Lisa explained about her foot. "I think I've re-injured it just a few minutes ago. I felt something crunch and pain shot up my leg."

"I don't have any x-ray equipment here, but if you can get into town I'll take a look at your ankle. What's the name?"

"Lisa Miller. I can be in town in about ten minutes...."

"Lisa Miller? The writer? Why didn't you tell me it was you? I was your doctor when you were just a little bitty thing. Of course, come right in dear. I'm looking forward to seeing you again." The doctor hung up then, before Lisa had a chance to ask any more questions.

She was met at the end of the sidewalk by a tall slender woman in her early seventies with dark gray hair, braided and wound into a bun at the back of her neck. Her face was smooth, unwrinkled, her eyes bright, and her step strong and sure. Before her she pushed a shiny wheelchair. "Into the wheelchair young lady. We don't want you doing anything else to that foot. I'd heard you were in town. Also heard you were in some kind of accident....suffering from amnesia and were here trying to regain your memory. Come inside, I'll bet there 's all kinds of questions you want to ask me."

Obediently Lisa hopped into the chair and waited as the doctor pushed her toward a cozy house nestled behind a beautiful garden. Every kind of flower she had ever seen was growing in the front of the cream colored two story house. Taking a few moments the doctor pointed out her prized rose garden. "That tall red one over there is my baby. I developed the color myself. It took first place two years ago in the rose competition for the western United States."

Through the front door Lisa was greeted by a large golden retriever. The dog sniffed her hand and growled deep in her throat. "Easy Maxine. This is a friend. " Even with these words the dog continued to look at Lisa threateningly...Finally the old dog walked slowly into the other room. "Sorry, she's getting old and cranky."

"We're going in here," the doctor pushed open a glassed and curtained door. On the other side was an examining table and shelves of medication behind a sturdy reinforced glass door.

"Can you get up on the table Lisa?" Doctor Mary steadied her while she climbed onto the table. Gentle hands removed her thick sock and unwrapped the ace bandage from the splint on her ankle. The doctor smiled, "You really did a number on this foot. What did you do, fall from the hay loft again?"

Lisa laughed, "Yes, actually I did. When did I do this before?"

"When you were about thirteen, I think. You were playing in the hay loft and fell from about half way up. You had a bad sprain then. It took two months for it to heal completely." Turning the foot gently the doctor watched the pain filled expression on her face. "Sorry. I suspect you've been on this foot too much, but other than that it looks about the way I' d expect it to."

Rewrapping the foot she replaced the brace and pulled the sock back on. "I want you to stay completely off this foot for the next two days. You can still get up to go to the bathroom, that sort of thing, but use your crutches. Soak the foot in very warm water twice a day and keep it elevated. Take two ibuprofen every four hours. A half an hour before you get up in the morning, take two of these. " She handed Lisa a bottle of pain pills. "If your ankle doesn 't start feeling better in three days, give me another call."

Helping her from the table and back into the wheelchair she asked if Lisa would like some iced tea. "I make a tea with raspberry, lemon and honey flavors I think you might find refreshing."

Holding onto her crutches Lisa frowned, "That's funny. Luke Sammons said that was his recipe."

Snorting the doctor turned a worried look toward Lisa, "That sounds like something Luke might pull. Have you been seeing him very much?"

Lisa explained about her injury and about Luke offering to take care of her. " But he was a little too overbearing and I felt I didn't really need anyone with me. I finally convinced him to go home. He fixed me a pot of hot tea before he left. He said it was his recipe." She didn't mention the near rape, or the dream, or whatever it was.

Nodding the doctor pushed her into a comfortable front room and helped her into an overstuffed chair and pushed close an ottoman to rest her foot on. "That young man has a lot of problems honey. You need to stay away from him. Let me get your drink and we'll talk."

The rest of the afternoon was spent in the comfortable living room. She started with the day Lisa was born and told her everything she could remember about her and her family. Up until the time she turned eighteen, Lisa had been under Doctor Mary's care. She'd seen her through the chicken pox, a number of sprained ankles, a broken arm, even two cases of pneumonia. It was like hearing a story told about a stranger. Nothing meant anything to her, nothing brought back any memories.

Finally the doctor looked at her watch and smiled. "It's nearly time for supper... Why don't you stay and eat with me? There's something more you need to know, but my mouth is dry from all this talking and I'm getting hungry. You sit here and keep that foot up. It won't take me long."

Supper was a steaming bowl of clam chowder, small cucumber and tuna sandwiches and more of the ice tea. For dessert she served homemade raspberry sorbet. It was all delicious. As the doctor cleared the dishes away Lisa looked up at her and smiled..."I can't thank you enough for everything, especially the information about my family and me. I wish I could say all of this has helped me remember, but it hasn't."

"Maybe this will." Doctor Mary wiped her hands on a towel and took something from the top of the refrigerator. She handed Lisa a color photo portrait taken many years before.

In it a much younger Lisa and a beautiful baby girl about two years old, were seated in a chair. Lisa took the photo and smiled at the picture. "Is that really me? I look so young! Who is the baby?"

"Turn the picture over," Doctor Mary said softly.

Lisa read the writing on the back, "Doctor Mary—my daughter Kelly—age two years…"

Lisa felt the room start to tilt and looked up in shock. "My daughter. I had a little girl. Then I was pregnant when I left, like Luke told me. Do you know what happened to her?"

Doctor Mary took the picture. "I received that picture in the mail about three months before your babysitter kidnapped your little girl. It was in all the papers, how you had hired this mature nurse to care for your little girl while you went to school. You came home one day and found all of the baby's clothes, toys, and everything, including your daughter, gone. Your mother and father did all they could to help you find her, but there was never a clue as to what had happened to her. You nearly went nuts, excuse the slang. It took you a long time to get over loosing her.

"Just before your parents were killed in an auto accident they contacted me. They wanted to know if there was a definitive blood test that could identify a child to its parents. I told them there was. They never said, but I always have thought they may have found Kelly. She would have been ten about then."

Lisa was stunned. A daughter….and such a pretty little girl too. Blonde, dainty, petite. She looked like a little angel. "Did I tell you who the father is?"

Doctor Mary stood up and walked over to the fireplace. She stood there for long minutes…"This is where the story gets kind of messy. Luke and Louis lived with their mother just a few blocks from here. After their father was killed, when they were about six, Mrs.

Sammons went a little crazy. Remember me telling you Luke Sammons has a lot of problems? His mother was his biggest one. For some reason she felt compelled to control the twins in every way she could think of. Luke went along with it, even as a child, but Louis rebelled. I don't know how many times he came to me in the night, crying and frightened and covered with welts where she had taken a switch or light cord, or whatever she could find to his back side. Those were in the days before Child Protection Services. Unless a child was being sexually abused or horribly neglected, the welfare department chose not to get involved. Louis begged me not to say anything to anyone. I was afraid if I did he would quit coming to me for help when he needed it. I often worried how the abuse would affect him as an adult, but I kept my mouth shut."

"He grew up to be a very handsome and gentle young man,in spite of it all, and you two fell in love during your senior year in high school. Everyone in town was pleased, except for the mother of the two boys. She was determined to do everything she could to break you two up. I always thought it was her behind what Luke did..." Doctor Mary came and sat down next to Lisa and took her hand. "The boys are identical twins, as alike in appearance at that time as any two twins I've ever seen. One night Luke showed up at your door pretending to be Louis. You fell for it. I think the mother must have been coaching him in order for him to be more like his brother. By then you and Louis had become more than just kissing boyfriend and girlfriend. Anyway, Louis walked in on you and his brother making love. There was a big fight, Louis beat the hell out of Luke. The mom was enraged. She blamed you for the whole thing, said you had been coming on to Luke."

Doctor Mary handed the picture back to Lisa. "A few weeks later you found out Kelly was on the way. You wanted me to do an in-utero blood test to tell who the father was, but with the boys being identical twins...."

"....there was no way to tell which one was the father," Lisa finished...She had a bad taste in her mouth as she thought of the diabolical deceit.

Doctor Mary nodded, "Exactly. Louis couldn't stand what his brother had done to you and he couldn't stand the thought you might be carrying his brother's child. You had a bitter quarrel and then shortly after that you left town. Your parents told me they sent you to finish school in another town in Idaho. You would have your baby there. Shortly after graduation Louis packed his things into his beat up old truck and left town. No one has heard from him since."

Lisa rubbed her forehead, "I have. Several times. And each time I see him he scares me to death." She went on to tell the doctor how the very sight of Louis sent terror through her.

"It may have something to do with your accident, or something that happened just before your accident. I can't imagine Louis doing anything to harm anyone, except maybe his brother. It's just not his nature. But….time has a way of changing people, it's hard to say how he would act now." They were quiet then for many minutes. Lisa was shocked at all the doctor had told her, but thankful for her frankness.

Doctor Mary looked at her watch again. "It's getting kind of late, honey. Would you mind if we continued this some other time?"

Pulling her crutches under her Lisa stood. She thanked the doctor for the help, the supper and the information. Following her out to her rented car the doctor held the door open for her while she settled herself under the wheel. Just before she started the car, Lisa asked Dr. Mary how Mrs. Sammons had died.

"A few years ago she contracted cancer. She was in a lot of pain, but it was operable and her prognosis was good. When she came home from the hospital she was on some heavy duty pain pills as the operation was very painful. Luke found her dead one morning, from what he claimed was an accidental overdose."

Dr. Mary stepped back from the car. "There was a lot of suspicion at the time. We found a pot of my hot raspberry tea next to her bed, in the bottom of her cup was grains of undissolved pain pills. We also found the pill bottle next to the pot. The prescription had just been filled, but the bottle was empty. Mrs. Sammons had a problem swallowing pills, always had. I gave Luke the recipe for the tea…With the fruit flavors in the tea, Mrs. Sammons couldn't taste the medication... Luke used to give his mother her pills like that all the time. There was inquiry into her death but nothing was ever proven."

Chapter Nine

Choking and gasping for air she woke. Sitting up she put her hand to her throat and tried to make her lungs work. She'd had a dream about traveling alongside the river again. She had wakened unable to breath.

Slipping from the bed she walked carefully to her bathroom. Getting a drink of water she went back to her bed. Sitting on the side of it she managed to calm herself.

It had been a week since her visit with Dr. Mary. Her foot was finally starting to heal, Janet had called and had been warned about what Beth had told her, and Beth was asleep in one of the upstairs bedrooms. It was early in the morning, barely six o'clock her bedside clock told her. Outside her window she could hear the cheerful chirping of songbirds greeting the day. Walking to the window she pulled the drapes open and looked outside.

Alongside the house grew a number of old apple trees. Close to her bedroom window one tree held a nest of fledgling robins just about ready to fly. She enjoyed watching their progress and spent many minutes each morning noting how close to leaving the nest the three little birds were. It wouldn't be long now before they would soar away into the sky.

Limping into the kitchen she poured water into a drip coffee maker and turned it on. Beth was an early riser, up before seven each morning. A coffee addict she had to have a hot cup of caffeine to get her day started. Each morning she groped her way to the kitchen, her eyelids barely open. Stirring her favorite instant coffee into a cup she would stumble to a chair and sit down. Both hands encircled the cup like a fond embrace. With each sip of the steaming brew her eyes opened a little farther until finally she was fully awake.

Lisa didn't drink coffee, she preferred tea. A compromise between the two was a ready pot of hot water and each could have their own brew.

Pouring herself a glass of orange juice Lisa limped back to her bedroom. While she showered she thought about her best friend. She was a character, that was for sure, but she was kind hearted and generous. When she saw Lisa on crutches she' d scolded her and told her she should have called. Beth was that way. She was concerned about her friend.

This was Beth's second morning here at the house. They had spent their first day exploring the town Lisa now called home. They had driven by all the public buildings in town, even stopping at the library. Every book Lisa had written was on its shelves but that did little to sway Beth's opinion of Adams. All the way back to the house Beth complained about small town living. She was just not impressed, she told Lisa over and over and wanted to know when Lisa would be returning to Vancouver.

"I don't know Beth," Lisa sighed. "I like it here and lately it's begun to stir up something in my head. Maybe it's because I'm relaxed and happy and...." she turned to her friend, "I've been trying to write. I have something I want you to look at....tell me what you think."

From her bedroom she brought the handwritten copy of a story she'd been working on. A fictional piece based on herself and the fear, frustration, and problems she was facing as an amnesiac.

Beth read the copy and smiled, "That's my girl! This is more like the old Lisa. How long have you been working on this?"

Lisa told her a few days.

"Why don't you use your computer? I saw your laptop in the bedroom. It would be a lot easier for you," Beth said as she looked toward Lisa 's room.

"I....ah....don't know how to hook it up," Lisa admitted. "When we got here I took it out and set it on the desk in my room, but didn't know how to connect it to the printer. Besides, I don' t know if I can type."

"You can. Better than I can." Beth took another sip. "As soon as I'm finished with my coffee I'll set the thing up for you. Then I'll show you how to use it."

From the day room Lisa could hear the gentle hum of the machine and she smiled. The typing had come back to her quickly. Words spilled out of her mind and onto the screen with ease. Page after page scrolled onto the screen of her computer. Beth read everything she wrote making suggestions and corrections as she wrote. She loved the story and Lisa loved writing it. It was getting easier for her every time she sat down at the keyboard. In the early morning and late evening she found she did her best work. Before Beth woke up she wanted to write a few things she 'd been thinking about.

Before she could get comfortable at her computer the tiny phone rang at her elbow. Picking it up she was pleased to hear Janet's voice. "Sorry it's so early, but we....ah....I mean....I have some plans for today and I wanted to talk to you before we left. Are you and Beth going to be at the farmhouse today? I thought Frankie and I would come to visit."

Lisa smiled with delight, "Sure we plan on being here. But how will you get here? You don't drive. Are you going to take the bus?"

Janet laughed a merry laugh. "No. A friend will drive us. I miss you Lisa...Is it all right if Frankie and I come to visit for a few days? And can my friend stay too?"

Of course it was all right. The rooms upstairs still held some of her things and Lisa admitted she missed them too. They'd find room for her friend. Janet promised they'd be there by lunch.

"Don't worry about fixing anything. I'll bring stuff with me to cook. I'll see you soon."

Setting the phone down Lisa had to admit Janet sounded optimistic. The lawyer must have given her good news. Turning to her computer screen she tried to gather her thoughts...An hour later she looked up to see Beth standing in the doorway, her ever present cup of coffee in her hand.

"Sorry. I didn't want to disturb you. How's the story coming ?" Placing her glasses on her nose she stood behind Lisa and read over her shoulder. "Good, good." She patted her friend' s back and settled into a comfy chair to finish her coffee.

Lisa was at the section of her story where she'd found out she had a child. This part was difficult for her. She had no memory of her daughter, could not remember how a mother feels about her child. But she had seen Janet and how she acted around her young son. Smiling, she used those memories to fill in the blanks. Pleased with her morning's work she pushed away from the computer.

"Don't forget to save your work," Beth called and took another sip of coffee.

Reaching for the mouse to save her work, a picture flashed through Lisa's mind. Trembling she looked at Beth and frowned. "This isn't the first time you've said that to me, is it!"

"Not for a long time," Beth suddenly looked up. "Have you remembered something?"

Lisa shrugged. "Not really, just an impression. What happened before?"

Beth put her cup down, "I bought you your first computer and taught you how to use it. At first you were always forgetting to save your work. You' d walk away from the keyboard and leave it for days. One time a power outage erased almost twenty pages of work. That's when I started nagging you about saving."

"I've been having mental flashes lately," Lisa stood up and stretched. "They're often out of context to what I' m doing and I have no idea what they mean. One flash in particular has me puzzled...I've had it several times in the last week. I'm standing at the front of a small white church, waiting. I feel like I'm suppose to be meeting someone, and I'm feeling very anxious."

"A wedding maybe?" Beth looked at her friend. "Did you go off and get married?"

Lisa laughed nervously, "Of course not. There would be a groom somewhere in the picture if I had."

It was close to one thirty when the dark 4x4 vehicle pulled into the driveway. Lisa frowned until she saw who was in the passenger seat. Smiling brightly Janet jumped out of the cab and ran to Lisa. Throwing her arms around her she grinned. From the driver side of the pick-up came Tom Cullens. In his arms he held Frankie.

Janet turned to Lisa and smiled, "Lisa, I'd like for you to meet my husband…."

Gasping with pleasure she first hugged Janet then pulled Tom into a group hug. She felt tears in her eyes. Then everyone started talking at once until finally Tom whistled through his fingers and made the women settle down. "Let's go inside. This little guy is wet!"

While Janet changed Frankie's diaper and clothes she explained quietly. Tom was wandering around looking at every thing in the house while his bride told Lisa and Beth how he and his fiancé had decided to split up. "She couldn't handle the thought he already had a child. I didn't know anything about it until he showed up at the apartment one night. He came to talk. The next morning he was still there, talking. We discovered we still cared about each other very much. It was like we'd never been apart."

Tom grinned at Janet. "I was still in love with her. I had done a pretty good job of convincing myself I wasn't but the moment I saw her in that deli I knew I was lying to myself. Any way we caught a shuttle to Reno and found a chapel…We've been married for three days." He kissed the side of her head.

"What did the lawyer have to say about this?" Lisa asked.

"Well….he accused us of being impetuous and living for the moment, but he said it was the best thing we could have done as far as the custody battle over Frankie is concerned. However, there is a fly in the ointment." Tom said quietly…"We think Janet's mother has found out that she was living in your apartment. We thought there was someone following us a couple of times and Janet said the phone would ring and then whoever is on the other end hangs up when she answers.

We talked to the lawyer and he advised us to stay away from the apartment for a while. We have a court date in a week. Chances are we will win our petition without any problems. But to avoid the possibility of the welfare department charging in and snatching Frankie away, he suggested we come here."

Janet was still grinning when she turned to Lisa. "I hope that's all right with you."

Lisa nodded. "Of course it is! I'm so happy for you two."

It didn 't take long for Janet to take over the massive kitchen again. Tom hovered around her, handing her items she needed while Frankie played contentedly on the floor. Janet fixed a huge supper of strogonoff, baby peas and onions in butter sauce, crescent rolls, green salad, and apple pie ala mode. Everyone pushed away from the table, too full to even talk.

Helping Janet clear the table Lisa carried an armful of dishes into the kitchen. On the counter lay the picture Dr. Mary had given her. Janet found it and picked it up..."Is this you Lisa? Who is that little girl?"

"I guess she's my daughter," Lisa explained. She told Janet about her visit with her old family doctor and everything she'd told her...Janet was looking at the picture closely, her face pulled into a frown.

She sat down hard in a chair. Wordlessly she pulled her wallet from her handbag, her hand trembling. She pulled out a picture and handed it to Lisa.

Looking at the pictures in her hands Lisa was puzzled. How was this possible? In her hands she held a wallet portrait of a child that looked just like the little girl in the Doctor's picture. "Where did you get this?"

Janet dropped her head and stared at the floor, afraid to look at Lisa. "That 's one of the baby pictures my mother had taken of me." They stared at the two nearly identical pictures for a long time.

Finally Janet said, "Mom told me I was almost three when I was adopted by her and my father. Dad died shortly after that from complications from diabetes. Mother ended up raising me by herself."

Stunned, Lisa joined Janet at the table. What were the chances that fate would have brought these two together after all this time? The odds were too immense to even think about. Shakily Lisa looked at her young friend. "Do you have any memories of your real mother?"

"Only one," Janet said softly. "I remember one birthday where my mother is giving me a birthday party. All I can remember is the cake. A clown cake with two candles."

"We need to investicate this before we jump to conclusions. Not that I wouldn 't love the idea, but we need to be sure. Have you got a picture of your mother?"

Janet pulled out a color photo of a woman in her mid-forties. She was pinched face and unsmiling. "This was taken about ten years ago. Since then her hair has gone completely gray and she's lost a lot of weight."

Staring at the picture Lisa shuddered. The face reached out to her, made her feel uneasy, a feeling of knowing this person was very strong for a moment then was gone. Shaking her head she tried not to stare. "I feel like I know this person....from somewhere."

Tom wandered into the kitchen about then and looked at the two women. Lisa took the pictures from Janet and smiled at the newly weds. Janet grinned at her husband and held out her hand, "Hi honey. How's Frankie doing?"

"He fell asleep over his ice cream. I put him down on the couch in the family room. Is there anything I can do to help in here?" He pulled Janet to him and kissed her cheek. "Are you all right? You look upset."

"I'm fine, just a little tired. If you really want to help we'll chase Lisa out of the kitchen and you can help me do the dishes." Janet started rolling her husband's sleeves up.

Preoccupied Lisa didn't argue. Turning to leave the room she looked at Tom quizzically when he made a strange statement.

"I feel like I know this place. I worked with this supervisor a few months ago that described a place like this in great detail. He was hoping to marry his childhood sweetheart and bring her back to her childhood home. Things must not have worked out like he planned.

Too bad. He really seemed to be in love with his lady." Pulling Janet to him he smiled at her, "but not as in love as I am with this lady."

Her head was swimming when she let herself into her room. Could Janet be her daughter? There was a slim possibility. Was that the reason she'd been in Lewiston County so many months before? How had she found out about Janet? Who told her ? How had she traveled there? Puzzled and confused she sat watching the robins as they tested their wings. Suddenly a quick breeze sent one of the little birds into the air. Flapping his wings he soared into the afternoon sun.

Finally she walked into her bedroom and began to pack an overnight bag. She needed a good private investigator. And she needed some privacy. She'd find neither in Adams. Beth was leaving tomorrow. She'd take the rented car back to Jim and catch a ride with her back to Vancouver. She'd tell Janet she needed to talk to a publisher there about her new book.

Jim was surprised when she pulled up in front of the service station the next morning. "I was just gettin' ready to call ya. Your car is finished."

Inside the bay stood her gleaming white convertible. Every trace of the mishap had been systematically removed. Her BMW looked and smelled like new. More than satisfied with his work Lisa beamed at Jim. Handing him a check he looked at her quizzically...

"A tip," she explained, "for doing such a beautiful job."

Stepping back outside she waved Beth on, "Go ahead Beth. I'll see you at the apartment tomorrow."

There was a lot of time to think on the trip back to Vancouver. Somehow she had to keep this to herself, not tell anyone until she had some answers. More than anything she didn't want to get Janet's hopes up. And to be honest with herself, she didn't want to be disappointed either. By the time she pulled into the underground parking at her apartment she was ready to call every Private Investigator in the book until she found one that could help her.

Stepping out of her car she locked the doors and turned to the elevator. A card key was necessary to gain entry to the elevator. The only other way was to take the stairs to the floor where the security guard was stationed. The card-key was missing from her purse. As was the key to her apartment. Searching her handbag she was afraid she'd left them at the house in Adams.

Limping and grumbling to herself she climbed the stairs and made her way to the guard. He smiled at her immediately, "Miss Miller. So good to see you."

"Could you let me into my apartment, Richard? I seem to have left my card-key and apartment key at the house in Adams."

"Not a problem, Ms. Miller. I'll call the super and he'll be glad to let you have a set of loaner keys."

In a few minutes the superintendent was waiting at her door. He unlocked it and handed her the key along with an elevator key-card. Assuring him she would return the keys before she left for Adams, Lisa stepped into her apartment.

Locking the door she flipped on the light switch and kicked off her shoes. The apartment was still stunningly beautiful to her. All the antique glassware, the perfectly matched and coordinated furnishings and accents. A showcase. But it didn't feel like home. The house in Adams did.

Sitting down on the overstuffed couch she reached for the phone book and found the listings for several private investigators. She set up two appointments. One of the two would surely be able to help her. Maybe she'd hire them both. Turning on the TV she walked into the kitchen and dug around in the freezer. In the door of the freezer she found several small dinners that Janet had prepared and set aside for her. Across the top was the heating instructions. Popping the dish into the microwave she set it and went back to the front room.

It was a quiet afternoon and evening. She watched a couple of programs on the TV and Beth called. Explaining about the missing keys Beth offered to let Lisa borrow her set, if she'd meet her at the office tomorrow morning. "Do you remember where it is?" Lisa didn't. Beth quickly gave her instructions.

"I'll see you tomorrow around nine," Lisa said and hung up.

Deciding to pack a few more of her clothes to go back to Adams with her, Lisa turned to her closet. Pulling down a large suitcase she started going through the many outfits and separates still hanging in her closet. She'd been working about forty-five minutes when she thought she heard the front door open. Thinking Beth had decided to bring the keys over that night she called, "I'm in here! Come on into the bedroom."

With her back to the door she didn't see him come into the room, didn' t have a clue he was there, until she felt his hand clamp tightly on her mouth. Kicking and struggling she tried to break loose from his grip, but it was like iron...He pulled her away from the closet and forced her into the front room. Throwing her down on the couch he stood away from her.

"Why did you decide to come back here? I thought this would be the one place no one would be able to find me. I've been waiting for close to a week for those youngsters to leave...." Luke's voice was brittle and full of panic. His eyes rolled from side to side and his mouth was pulled into an ugly sneer. One eye was blackened and swollen, there was a crusty cut across his lower lip and a large yellowed bruise colored his right cheek. Looking at her, his eyes narrowed. "You told the police what I did, didn' t you! They'll be here in a little while to arrest me!"

Lisa shook her head violently. "No! No! I didn't! I didn' t know you were here! Besides....I couldn't tell....if what happened was a dream or real. No one knows you're here Luke, really."

His eyes narrowed again, "A dream? What are you talking about?"

Scrambling to her feet, she backed away from him until she felt the back of her legs against one of the tables scattered around her front room. Groping behind her she felt the heavy purple bowl on the table. Her hand closed over the rim of it. "When you stayed with me that night I guess I took too many pills and everything about that night became like a dream to me. I had a nightmare, a bad dream where someone tried to attack me, but I don't know who it could have been. In fact, I thought you had rescued me."

He snorted…"Rescued you? That rich." Facing her he tried to smile but only deepened the sneer. "It's just that I've always been in love with you. When my brother could have you any time he wanted, I couldn't stand it. Mom understood. I had to know what it was like to have you…. to touch you and hold you….to make love with you. The other day I thought maybe it could be the way it was that night so long ago, when you thought I was Louis…"

He started to cry then. "When we found out you were pregnant I wanted to tell you the truth, but mother wouldn't let me. I saw her once, your little girl, when you didn't know I was near. She was such a pretty little thing. I really wished things were different then…."

He sat down and rubbed his temples. "Then that awful woman you had for a babysitter stole your little girl and I saw how hurt you were on the news. I was so sorry…Years later after mother died I talked to Louis on the phone and told him the truth. I begged him to forgive me…."

Lisa stood very still. She didn't know what to do or how to act. Her hands behind her back she waited. Surely something would happen that would give her a hint as to handle this. The chance came a few moments later. Luke stood up and wiped the tears from his face. Walking to the window he looked down at the boats on the river.

"It's so beautiful here. I've always wanted an apartment like this. Mother said I had to stay with her, to be safe. But I could have lived in a place like this." He turned his back to her. Now was her chance.

Picking up the bowl she prayed for a good aim and threw the heavy dish as hard as she could…Just at that moment he turned to face her and the bowl barely grazed him. Crashing into the heavy safety glass the window cracked noisily but did not break through…

"Why did you do that!" he screamed at her and lunged. He was on her in two steps, his hands around her throat. For endless minutes they seemed to dance around the room, crashing into one table then another. He slammed her head against a window frame and she felt a dark void pulling at her. She couldn't breath, was loosing her strength and slumped down to the floor.

Suddenly his hands were no longer on her throat. Her eyes wouldn't focus and her ears were filled with wild screaming. Above her she could vaguely make out the form of two men struggling. One of the men grabbed the other through the legs and around the waist and hoisted him into the air. With a terrible crash the man went flying into the cracked glass window, and through it into the dark night. Below she heard a sickening thud as the body bounced off the decorative rocks below, then a muted splash as he fell into the river.

She was panting, trying to breath. Someone knelt beside her and she could see his blue eyes and his handsome face. She smiled at him then lost consciousness.

Chapter Ten

It was dark when she woke up, her head bandaged and her throat raw. She looked around the room for him but he wasn't there. Buzzing the nurse she asked with a rasping voice, "Is my husband still in the hospital?"

"Yes he is Mrs. Sammons. Shall I find him and send him to your room?"

"Yes, please. Tell him to bring me something cold to drink, my throat is really raw."

In moments his handsome face was over hers. "Hi honey, I'm glad you're finally awake. How are you feeling?"

She tried to raise the head of her bed, but wasn't able to see the button. He pushed it and brought her head up slightly. "I feel better, I guess." She smiled at him and took a sip of the soft drink he offered her.

Taking a seat on the edge of the bed he nodded then smiled down at her. "I'm glad you're finally awake....I was beginning to think you were never going to come back to me."

Shuddering slightly she answered weakly, "I guess I came pretty close to dying."

He nodded and picked up her hand. Kissing her fingers he slipped a diamond and gold ring onto her left hand. "I found this the other day and thought it should probably be put back where it belongs."

Lifting her hand she smiled at the wedding ring. "It's beautiful. It does look good there."

A nurse came into the room and smiled at them. "You'll have to leave Mr. Sammons, but you can come back in a few minutes. We just want to change her bandages, clean her up and change her bedding. Give us about twenty minutes."

Nodding he stood and leaned over her then gently kissed her lips.

Startling awake Lisa looked around her. Another dream? She was in a hospital bed again, her head wrapped with a bandage but there was no Louis in her room and no ring on her finger. Pushing her call button she waited for the nurse.

While she waited she realized her memory had returned. With mounting excitement she remembered being ten and falling from a horse. She broke her arm that day and everyone at school had signed her cast. She remembered going on a long trip with her parents and thinking they'd never get where they were going. Suddenly she was at Disneyland and headed for the best vacation she'd ever had.

She remembered her parents, her mother so petite, blonde and pretty. Her father so dark and strong…People told her she looked like her father and she didn't mind. She loved her daddy.

School had always been easy for her and writing especially came easy. She was chosen as the most likely to publish a best seller by her classmates her senior year. She remembered the argument with Louis and how it hurt to have him look at her. She remembered leaving school and being pregnant. She remembered the day her little girl was born and how painful her birth had been and how frightened and alone she felt. And she remembered the feeling of despair, the pain of discovering the kidnapping and knowing her child was gone. Years later she remembered the pain of loosing her parents, the awful accident that had taken their lives.

All of her childhood memories had returned and she reveled in them. She went back through them again and again. There were tears in her eyes when the nurse came to her room. Asking how long she'd been in the hospital she was told she was brought in the night before.

"You have a slight concussion, but the doctor that examined you said you could probably go home today," the nurse offered as she tidied the bed and filled her water pitcher.

"How did I get here?"

"Evidently you were attacked by someone in your apartment and the neighbors heard and called the police. The officer responding found you in the front room below a broken glass window....said you must have pushed your assailant out the window somehow. They haven't found a body, it must have fallen in the river. Are you hungry? Breakfast was served about an hour ago, but I can have the kitchen send up something for you."

Lisa shook her head, "Has anyone been in to ask about me?"

At the door the nurse looked back at her and smiled, "Your friend Beth was here last night and again this morning. She asked we call and let her know when you woke up. And an absolutely gorgeous man was in this morning and asked about you...I've never seen such beautiful blue eyes!"

Everyone was excited about Lisa's memory returning. Beth grinned and said now there was no reason for her not to finish that manuscript. Janet and her husband grinned and silently figured they need not feel guilty about getting on with their lives. There was still a lot of blank spots in her memory, but almost daily she was remembering more and more.

One blank that puzzled her was why she was in Lewiston county. She still had no idea why she was in that part of the country and how the accident had occurred or where or why. Could that part of her life have something to do with Janet?

It was early afternoon two days later when she approached the door of the Private Investigator...Knocking, she let herself in and looked around. The office was nothing like the ones she'd seen on television and she smiled secretly at the stereotype...The office was neat, but very small. There were several filing cabinets, a desk, three or four comfortable looking chairs, a nice thick carpet on the floor, and another door leading into a....restroom? The voice apologized from behind the door and asked her to be seated.

Wiping his hands on a paper towel he came into the room. He was tall, over six foot, tanned and ruggedly good looking. He was wearing a shirt, tie, and trousers. His brown eyes sparkled when he introduced himself.

"I'm Fred Norrise," he said and shook her hand. Pulling out a chair he offered her a seat. "What is it you need an investigator for Ms. Miller?"

"I'm looking for my daughter. About eighteen years ago she was kidnapped from me by her babysitter. I'm looking for an investigator that will help me locate her. I talked to another gentleman this morning and was told my case was hopeless. I hope you can be a little more encouraging." Lisa looked at her purse. Inside were the two pictures she'd borrowed from Janet.

He nodded silently and made notes while she explained to him what she wanted him to do. Find out about Janet's adopted mother. If possible find out about Janet 's natural mother, and if he could, find out where Louis Sammons was at...Somehow he tied into all of this. Smiling he agreed to take her case. He would do the best he could. He would contact her as soon as he had something to report...

Lisa was subpoenaed by the court about her stolen car. Reluctantly she returned to Jerome for the day and waited her turn to testify. At the defendant's table she saw the young boy, his hair long, black and greasy, hanging over his dark eyes...He never smiled, never showed any emotions. Behind him his parents sat, whispering encouraging words to him.

Her testimony lasted only a few minutes. She hadn't actually seen the car taken by Kyle, she admitted, but his family had approached her several days later to try to settle out of court. The judge nodded and made notes.

Before the trial was over Lisa discovered Kyle had been in more trouble than his parents would ever admit to. He'd been implicated in several house break-ins in the Jerome area but without enough evidence, couldn't be tried on those crimes. This was his third car theft, but his first trial. He was an admitted drug user and had been found carrying meth when he was arrested. The boy's habit was not supported by the lavish allowance his indulgent parents had given him. He was in constant trouble with the law and had a list of crimes several sheets long.

As the defendant stood to hear the verdict of the judge, Mr. Lamont looked over at Lisa and glared. There was so much malice in that look it made her uncomfortable. It was no surprise the judge found the boy guilty on every charge. He would be held over for sentencing. Mrs. Lamont collapsed into a chair, her husband standing above her unable to comprehend what had just happened.

Driving home Lisa wondered what could have turned that boy into such a hoodlum. Obviously his parents spoiled him and used their money and influence to keep him out of trouble...But there didn't seem to be a speck of human decency about him. That, along with the drug use, was probably the reason little Kyle was looking at doing some hard time in prison.

Sighing wearily Lisa pulled into her driveway at the house. She only needed to pick up her bag before she headed back to Vancouver. Climbing the stairs she couldn't help but think now the boy may actually get the help he needed.

Back on the road in less than thirty minutes, Lisa soon lost herself in her thoughts. Suddenly the little phone inside her purse began to ring. Digging it out she turned it on and listened.

It was a man's voice talking but she was having a hard time understanding what he was saying. Finally she told the caller to speak up.

"It's not over....someone you care about will pay!"

Shocked, Lisa turned the phone off and threw it onto the seat beside her. The rest of the trip back to her apartment she couldn't shake a feeling of doom.

The custody hearing date was coming up fast. They were ready. Everyone was anxious for it to be over with. Lisa, Beth, Janet, Frankie and Tom along with their lawyer met in the lobby of the court house about an hour before the hearing. They expected Janet's mother to be there with a troop of lawyers. Expecting a full blown war, they were surprised when Janet's mother didn't put in an appearance. The judge listened to the petition and asked if there was any contest to it. There being none, Frankie became Janet and Tom's legal ward.

In celebration the group went to a fancy lunch in the restaurant of the swank Liberty Hotel. Raising his glass of tea Tom toasted his family and their triumph. "Here's to us and all of our loved ones! May we always find happiness. God bless the lawyer!"

Everyone drank a toast then Tom turned to Janet, "You going to tell them, or should I?"

Janet giggled and blushed, "I guess I'll tell them the good news. We just found out this morning....we're going to have another baby."

Clapping and congratulating the young couple, no one saw the woman come up to the booth. Her face was contorted with anger, her mouth pulled down in a hateful frown. Dressed in a black pants suit that hung from her thin frame she looked wasted and frail...Standing to the side it was several moments before she caught Janet' s eye.

"Mama?" Janet whispered.

Tom felt her grip his arm. Turning toward the angry woman the smile quickly left his face..."Mrs. Napp? What are you doing here?"

"I've come to get my kid!" she reached for the baby but Lisa was faster and had Frankie out of his chair and into her lap before the woman could put her hands on him. Holding him close she turned away from Mrs. Napp, shielding him.

Disoriented, Mrs. Napp looked at the group curiously. "They told me you were here, those people on the phone. They said it would be easy to get my boy back...."

"I'm afraid that isn't going to happen, ma'am." Tom said quietly and stood up between her and the child. "Janet and I went to court today and Frankie is now legally our son, forever."

"Humph! Court! What do they know. They don't know how much work it is to raise a kid by yourself...." she seemed unaware of anyone but the baby and the girl cowering in front of her. "You didn't have no right to steal that baby from me, you little whore!"

"Hey! You can't talk to my wife that way!" Tom snapped and stepped even closer to the woman. "I think you'd better leave...In fact I suggest you leave right now, as I'm going to have the waiter call the police." Signaling a passing waiter Tom briefly explained their situation. The woman looked around her as if just awakening.

For the first time she looked right at Lisa. Her eyes widened with terror and she turned to leave. Lisa thought she had a moment of recognition but then she was unsure...Before she could respond the woman was gone. Running through the restaurant she was stopped by the manager at the door. Held firmly they could hear her screams of rage. The police arrived moments later and escorted the now babbling woman from the building.

"She'll probably be spending some time in a psychiatric ward," the manager assured the group. "We apologize for the incident. Your lunch is on us."

Shakily Janet gathered Frankie into her arms. Looking at Lisa gratefully she thanked her again and again for helping them. "She would have just taken him away and I would never have seen him again."

Just like what happened to me, Lisa thought to herself. "I wonder what she meant, someone calling her and tell her where we were."

No one could answer that question but Lisa suspected the Lamonts had something to do with it.

Solemnly everyone gathered their things to return to their vehicles. Janet and Tom told Lisa and Beth good-bye. "My construction job is finished here so we're returning home. I own this little farm outside Bend, Oregon. I think Janet is going to like it there."

Janet handed Lisa a small piece of paper, "I've written down our address and phone number in Bend. I hope you'll call and keep in touch."

It was a tear-filled good-bye. Frankie clung to Lisa and covered her face with his wet kisses. Standing on the curb, Beth and Lisa waved to the young couple until their taillights were lost in the swarm of traffic.

"They'll be fine," Beth assured her friend. "Those two really care for each other. Their house will be filled with love and happiness...And Frankie will have a little brother or sister! You gotta admit, kiddo, that should make you happy."

Lisa nodded. Sniffling she looked at her friend, "You're right. We all need to get on with our lives, now that I have mine back. I wish I could remember the accident, though. Then I wouldn't feel like there's such a big blank spot in the middle of my life."

Walking toward their cars Beth handed Lisa a business card. "My therapist. Maybe she can help."

It was hard to stay in the apartment, so soon after the attack and she wouldn' t have if there had been time to head back to Adams before dark. The window was securely boarded over and the superintendent promised the workmen would have the glass replaced before the end of the week. Even with that, Lisa pulled the heavy drapes hiding the ugly wood behind them. Somewhere around midnight she finally made it to her room and turned on her TV. Hoping to find a romantic love story or action film she flipped through the stations. Finding nothing of interest she turned the set off and picked up a book.

It was one she had written several years before. Reading through the first page, she smiled. She knew exactly what would happen in this story she could remember writing every word. Even the look of approval on Beth's face when she turned the manuscript over to her was recalled. Flipping through the book she sighed and slammed the cover shut. Turning off the bedside lamp she snuggled into her blankets...

Sleep came faster than she thought it would. She felt cozy, safe and drifted away into a dream state.

Around her were beautiful flowers; roses, daisies, carnations, lilies, gladiolus, every kind of flower found in a florist shop had filled her front room. She was laughing giddily and sniffing first one flower than another. A little white card in her hand asked for her forgiveness and gave a phone number.

Smiling she dialed the number. A man's voice, one she'd heard from long ago, answered, "Did you get my flowers?"

Laughing she slid into a chair and answered, "Yes. They're beautiful. But why so many?"

"I didn't know what kind you like the best, so I bought out the florist shop. Did you get the ones you like most?" His voice was tender and full of anticipation.

"I love them all," she whispered. "And yes I forgive you.... where are you?"

"Actually I'm across the street from your apartment building. I was hoping you might ask me to come over." The line was silent while she thought about it, for about five seconds.

"Yes. Come over. I'll call down to the security guard and let them know you're to be let in. I'll see you in a few minutes." Hanging up she called Richard at the desk and told him she was expecting company...

Minutes later she heard a gentle tapping and she went to the door. He was there, tall, dark, strong and smiling. Whisking her into his arms he picked her up and planted a tender kiss on her lips. "I've been waiting almost twenty years to do that. Do you mind?"

Her answer was another kiss. "I've been waiting a long time too," she whispered against his shoulder.

He carried her into the front room and sat down with her in his lap. Over the next few hours they talked, laughed and cried together. There were many years lost between them and they systematically brought each other up to date.

"About five years ago I saw your face on the cover of your first book and almost choked on my sandwich. I couldn't believe what seeing you again did to me. I knew then I'd been an idiot so long ago. It wasn't your fault. Can you truly forgive me for being so stupid?"

She kissed his cheek and whispered, "Long forgotten."

He looked deep into her eyes and frowned, "There is something you need to know, Lisa. It isn't going to be easy to hear. I talked to

Luke a few years back. He told me he's sterile, had been since he was thirteen. He had the mumps and they went down on him. I didn't remember how sick he'd been then. Mother never told me. The baby was mine."

She slid off his lap and stood up. All these years she'd hoped and prayed for something like this, an answer to who the father was of her child. She turned her back to him so he wouldn't see the tears. She felt him come up behind her and put his hands on her shoulders.

"I've been searching for you for a long time, to tell you. But, long before I knew the truth about the child, I knew how much I really cared for you…I've bought every one of your books, read them from cover to cover. With each book I was determined to find you. But your publishing company and your agent refused to tell me where you were! Then I got smart. I looked in the phone book. I had to go through about two hundred Lisa Miller's in seven different states before I finally found you." He turned her to face him. "Please believe me when I tell you I never stopped loving you. I was just too young and too stubborn to admit it."

They spent the night wrapped in each other's arms, talking. They talked about everything, what kind of work they both were doing, the successes of Lisa's books, where Louis had been. He told her he now owned a contracting company and was very successful in Idaho. Slowly the night turned to morning. By first light they agreed to try to find Kelly.

"It's kind of odd but maybe it's worth mentioning," he said as he accepted a cup of coffee from Lisa.

"What's that?"

"A while back I worked with this young guy that was going through hell. His girlfriend's mother was keeping him away from her. He'd written her, tried to call, even wanted to go back and see her but the mother wouldn't permit it. She insisted the girl didn't want to have anything to do with this young man. He was crazy about her and was going through all kinds of torment. The reason I mention it is because he showed me a picture of his girl and well….she looked like your mom did when I first knew you, almost identical to her."

"Where did she live?" Lisa asked, "Where....where....where....?"

The question echoed through her mind as her alarm clock brought her back to her real world. Slapping the alarm button she blinked. Sitting up she looked around the room. That wasn't a dream, she told herself, that was a memory.

Louis had come to her. They'd spent the night together and had been determined to find their child. But where was he now? Why did seeing him send such terror through her?

Walking into the bathroom she splashed cold water on her face. Picking up a towel from the counter top to dry her face, she knocked something small and golden off the edge of the sink. Stooping to pick it up she smiled, then felt a chill chase up her back. Slipping the ring on her left ring finger she held her hands to her chest. He would come to her again, she knew, and soon.

Chapter Eleven

Their footsteps echoed down the long corridor as the doctor led Lisa to a barred room..."You must understand we have not made any progress with Janice. She may try to turn on you suddenly, we aren't sure. The only reason I have agreed to try this is to help Janice. We can't seem to reach her, can't get her to respond to us. Perhaps seeing you will help us help her."

"Years ago she may have been the one that kidnapped my daughter. That was nearly eighteen years ago. I'm not sure if she is the one that did that. In a few minutes I should be able to tell." Setting her jaw firmly she waited as the doctor pulled out her keys to unlock the door.

"All right then. We'll be watching through the one way glass and we 'll be just outside the door. Try to stay out of her reach, she' s very quick." The key clicked and she pulled the heavy door open. "Good luck, Ms. Miller."

The room was completely padded, no furniture. In one corner sat the haggard figure of Mrs. Napp her gray hair smooth, her blue uniform tidy. She looked up at Lisa sadly as she came into the room. She made no move to come closer to her only watched her with mild interest.

"Hello Mrs. Napp. Do you remember who I am?" Lisa squatted down across the room from the woman, with the door to her back.

"Yes. I remember you. You're that writer." She continued to look at Lisa.

"That's right, Lisa Miller. I'm also Janet's friend...Do you remember Janet?" Lisa shifted her weight off of her still sore ankle.

"Yes. My daughter Janet, ungrateful little snot. After all I did for her and now look where I'm at!" Tears came to the woman's eyes..."Why did she do this to me? All I was trying to do was protect the child, nothing more. 'The sins of the father shall be visited on the child '. That's in the Bible. Frankie don't stand a chance with that woman...." her voice trailed off and she looked away from Lisa...Muttering under her breath Lisa was unable to hear what she said.

"I'm sorry Mrs. Napp, what did you say?" Lisa leaned forward..."When you were in the restaurant, do you remember the restaurant, I thought you recognized me. Can you tell me if I know you Mrs. Napp?"

Again she muttered under her breath. Her head turned away from Lisa, she couldn't understand what the woman was saying.

Stepping closer to the woman still sitting on the floor in the corner, Lisa edged closer to the pathetic woman. "I'm sorry Mrs. Napp, I can't hear you. Please turn around and look at me."

Slowly her head turned toward Lisa and the look on the woman's face sent a chilling shudder all through her body. Lisa backed away as the woman slowly stood up.

"I said Janet is just like her mother before her! Bitches! Whores!" She was uncoiling herself like a snake, ready to strike. Before she could move any closer to Lisa the Doctor was at the door with two strong orderlies.

Grabbing Lisa by the arms they pulled her out of the room. As Lisa heard the door slam behind her the woman inside began to rave at the top of her lungs. A string of obscenities followed her down the hall.

"I'm sorry," the doctor apologized, "I tried to warn you how unstable she is. She's been doing that with anyone who enters her room. She always fixes on her daughter's birth mother, calling her a whore. We're not sure, at this point, what that means. Did you get the answer you wanted?"

Lisa shook her head, "No. I can't be sure. If it is the same woman she's changed so much I don't recognize her."

The doctor smiled a weak smile at Lisa. "I guess we're back to square one...I don't think you should plan on seeing her again for a very long time..." Turning on her heels the doctor left Lisa standing in the hall and returned to her patients.

Fred's voice on the telephone was friendly but not very encouraging. "I 've found a few records about Janet, mostly school stuff, but Janice moved around a lot during Janet's early school years and there's nothing very substantial anywhere that I can find." She could hear papers rustling on the other end of the line. "There is one thing, though. A retired school teacher in the Boise area remembers Janet from the second grade. She remembers her telling a friend in her class that she thought she had been stolen. The friend then told the teacher but she thought it was an overly active imagination. When she tried to talk to Mrs. Napp about it, the woman refused to respond and the next day they were gone again. The teacher always wondered about that, so it stayed in her thoughts."

Fred reported to Lisa no records could be found of Janice Napp ever adopting a child. "As far as I can see the woman was a lie start to finish. There' s no record of her ever being married, ever adopting a child, nothing. She's one of those people who exist but not on paper."

They would have to try another lead. For days Lisa had been wracking her brain trying to remember the babysitter's name from so long ago. Finally in desperation she called Dr. Mary.

"Let me think, what was that woman's name." Dr. Mary was silent for a few minutes. "I think it was Julia something....Julia Noles! That 's it. Her name was Julia Noles!"

Lisa thanked the doctor and hung up. Quickly she redialed Fred's number. "See what you can find out about a Julia Noles. That's the name given to me when I hired the woman as my babysitter. She may have been a nurse." Again he told her he'd call as soon as he had something to report...

The workmen were hard at work replacing the window when she arrived back at her apartment. Smiling grudgingly she looked at the mess and called the apartment super. "I'm going back to Adams for a few days. Call when the window is finished, ok?"

It looked stormy when she pulled her car out of the garage and it wasn't long before fat rain drops splatted on her windshield. A few miles down the road the rain became a torrential downpour. It had been raining like this for days now and there were concerns about flooding in some of the lower areas. Flash flood warnings had been issued for parts of Idaho and Eastern Oregon. Cautiously Lisa made her way back to the little town.

Driving through Adams she wasn't surprised to see the power was off. No doubt the lines were down. Pulling through the streets she hurried on toward the house...The wind was blowing fiercely driving the rain in waves across the roadway. It was hard to see and although it was mid-day the sky was as dark as twilight.

Pulling off of the road leading to her house, she was horrified to see the old dead tree at the end of the driveway slowly teeter and fall across the lane, just in front of her car. Slamming on her brakes she couldn't avoid her car slipping into the heavy trunk of the tree. Suddenly her face was covered with a soft "whoosh" as the air bag inflated and deflated instantly. Snapping upright she looked around.

Terrified, she sat there shaking. She was unhurt and the damage to the car was minimal, but she was unable to move. A memory, something terrifying, was trying to edge itself into her conscious mind, but she fought against it. Holding her head with her hands she tried to drive away the images that danced before her closed eyes...

The driveway was several hundred feet long, graveled but muddy in a hard rain. Stepping out of her car she shut the door and turned her face into the wind. Running as quickly as her sore ankle would allow she made it to the front door. The torrential rain had drenched her and she felt chilled.

Finding her key she let herself into the dark house. Flipping a light switch she cursed when she remembered the lights were off. Pulling off her wet coat and muddy shoes she hurried to her room.

Not even the water worked, she realized as she tried to turn on a warm shower. The water pump ran off the same lines that powered the lights in the house. No gas generator had ever been installed. Shaking from the chill she pulled off her wet clothes and found a thick robe to wrap herself in. Walking to her day area she knelt beside the fireplace. She was shaking so hard she couldn't light the match to start the fire. Shaking and shivering she curled into a ball. A fitful sleep soon over took her.

She woke to a crackling fire. Her shivering had stopped and beside her was a hot cup of tea. Picking up the cup she drank the warm brew quickly. Sitting up on the couch she looked around. The electricity was still off but the fireplace sent a flickering light across the room.

"Ah, you're awake," he said as he came into the room with a tray. He set it on a table. Looking down at her he smiled, "Are you feeling warmer now?" In the dark his face was hidden, but not even the dark could hide the blue fire in his eyes.

She looked up at him, "Of course darling. But I'm feeling lonesome." She held open the blanket as an invitation.

Grinning he slipped into the warm afghan with her. She could feel his warmth, his strength and she put her arms around his neck. His lips were sweet on hers and it wasn't long before they kindled their own fire. She forgot to wonder why he was there.

Through the long dark night they held each other, talking little. Toward morning he turned to her and stroked her face gently. "My love, I must leave now. I'll be back soon. I'm glad you have remembered more, but you still have not remembered it all. Until you do we cannot truly be together."

She started to protest, to tell him how frightened she was, but he shushed her and put his finger to her lips, "Ssshh. It will be all right." Leaning over the bed he kissed her gently and slipped away. "Sleep now, my forever lover, I'll come to you again soon."

Drowsiness swept over her and although she fought it her eyelids closed. The next thing she knew the sun was pouring through her bedroom windows and the birds were noisily singing outside. Her cell phone was ringing in the other room where she' d dropped her purse. Grabbing her robe she hurried to answer it.

"Ms. Miller? This is Fred Norrise. Sorry to call so early but I thought you might like to know what I found. Julia Noles was listed in a nurse's roster. She was a bonified licensed practical nurse. She worked in the Dornbecker 's Hospital here in Portland for close to two years. She was dismissed because of inappropriate behavior. I've talked with the head nurse that was working at the time, and she remembered Julia. She said Julia couldn't keep her hands off the babies that were brought in. She was dismissed because the administration thought she was unbalanced. After Dornbecker's the trail leads to you then goes cold. No sign of her anywhere, but about the time Julia disappears Janice shows up." He was quiet for a moment. "Do you want me to keep searching? I mean, this is getting kind of spendy, I 'm not sure there's much more I can dig up."

"Keep searching." Lisa told him. "Find out if Janice suddenly appeared with a young girl, about two and half years old, blonde, petite. There must be a neighbor or someone somewhere that would remember her. I simply have to know if Janet is my daughter."

"Ok, I'll keep looking," he was quiet a moment. She heard his voice loose its professionalism and ask, "Are you all right Lisa? You sound different."

Rubbing her eyes she assured him she was all right, just tired.

"All right, I'll call in a few days and report what I have. I hope you get some rest!" he hung up then and she ran her fingers through her hair.

Looking around her she sighed. Her car still sat at the end of the driveway, resting up against the tree trunk. She would have to call Jim and have the air bags recharged...Then she would have to call someone to remove that tree. Picking up the local phone book she again called Jim's Service Station. Getting the number she needed from him she dialed it. The answering voice told her someone would be by that afternoon to remove the dead tree.

Sighing heavily she flipped the light switch and cursed softly when nothing happened. Looking up the number for the power company she dialed their number. She was told her lights should be back on within the hour.

She felt grungy not being able to shower, but she put on her clothes and walked to the kitchen...Finding yogurt, cookies and fresh fruit she made up a quick meal and sat down to eat it.

About half way through her banana the lights flickered back on. Placing her dishes in the sink, she turned to the bathroom. Filling the huge tub with lukewarm water she climbed in. The soapy, warm water felt heavenly and she put her head back against the rim of the tub. Closing her eyes she drifted away into a dream.

"Hand me the soap," he commanded and splashed her with water playfully..."I'll scrub your back for you."

Smiling wickedly she handed him the soap then grabbed his arm when he reached to take it..."I'll give you one minute to get out of your clothes and into the tub with me. Otherwise I'm going to drench you."

His eyes sparkled merrily as he slipped out of his clothes and joined her in the warm water...Pulling her to him he kissed her tenderly. She felt a fire beginning to glow and he smiled gently. Through his kisses he growled, "Woman you are going to wear me out!"

His hands were everywhere bringing sensations to her body that sent shivers of excitement all through her. His mouth left hers only long enough to taste her neck, her ear lobes, her shoulders. Finally she felt all reason leave her and felt him pull himself over her.

It became apparent almost immediately their position in a tub full of water was not the most opportune for love making. His passion was great, as was hers, but she became uncomfortable when the water splashed over her face with each movement they made...

"Ah....darling, maybe we should go into the bedroom," she whispered against his mouth. He didn't respond, only pulling her closer to him in his lust. Holding her breath helped a little but she lost interest in their lovemaking quickly.

It was as if he couldn't hear, or didn't want to. Whenever his body crashed into hers a wave of warm soapy water washed over her face, blinding her with stinging soap and making her gasp for air. Finally spent he pulled away from her and fell into the water beside her. She blinked the soap from her eyes and looked at him closely.

"I'm sorry," he said softly, "I just couldn' t stop. Are you all right?"

She stood up and looked down at him, "I'm fine. I don't think we'll be trying that again for a while, though." Reaching for a towel she felt her foot slip and she fell face first into the water of the massive tub.

Suddenly she couldn't breath, couldn't get out of the water. It had become dark, murky and cold. Clawing at the side of what used to be the tub she realized she was no longer in her bathroom but inside something else and it was under water...Her foot seemed to be tangled, holding her under the water. Too terrified to try to reason what had happened she suddenly found an opening and pulled herself through it. Kicking as hard as she cold she finally broke the surface just as she felt her lungs would burst.

He was still sitting in the tub watching her with a curious frown, "Honey? Are you all right?"

Gasping and choking she slid from the tub to the floor. Unable to talk for long rasping minutes she looked at him terrified, "Why didn't you help me? "

Shocked, his eyebrows shot up, "Honey you were only in the water a split second...Before I could respond, you had pulled yourself out. What's wrong?"

Still gasping for air she sat on the bathroom floor, the towel wrapped loosely around her. She sat there trembling, until her breathing became easier. A knock at the bathroom door brought her head up. Looking around the bathroom she was surprised to find herself alone, no sign of Louis anywhere. The water was now cold and covered with a thick soap scum.

"Who? Who is it?" she called hoarsely through the door and pulled the towel tighter around her.

"Lisa? Are you all right? I banged on the damn front door until my knuckles are raw. When you didn't answer I let myself in." It was Beth...

"Beth! I'll be right out. Just give me a minute." She stood up, found herself still trembling and reached for her thick terry cloth robe. Looking around the room again she opened her bathroom door.

Beth looked at her friend and frowned, "What the hell is going on with you kiddo ? You look like death warmed over. Haven't you been sleeping at night ?"

Lisa sat down on the edge of her bed, "I don't know Beth. I keep having these dreams."

Sitting beside her friend Beth smiled tenderly. "There's something not right here Lisa. Ever since the accident and you moved to this house you've been different. I know you're still having problems remembering everything, but I can tell you right now, you're acting weird. You're acting like you're on the verge of a nervous breakdown." Beth took Lisa's hand in her own. "Have you tried my therapist ? Why don't we call her and set up an appointment?"

"No, I'm all right. Let me get dressed and we'll talk." Lisa shook her head. "Why are you here?"

"I'm not really sure. I got this weird message on my answering machine...It sounded like you, sort of, except the person who called sounded sick or something..." Beth rubbed her forehead. "Whoever it was said you were in trouble and I should come right away. I tried to call you, but your phone must have been turned off. I drove out here as fast as I could. It took me only three hours instead of four. I'm lucky I'm not on the ten most wanted list."

Lisa stepped back into the bathroom and let the water out of the tub. Looking around the room she frowned. That dream, like a lot of others, had seemed real to her...Especially the part where she'd been unable to surface, had almost drowned...Louis had been there with her, as he had been in most of her dreams lately. Why was he only visiting her in her sleep? Trembling she fled the bathroom. She 'd have to sort all this out later.

Beth was chatting away fixing herself a cup of coffee. In her hand she held a hard copy of Lisa's latest manuscript. "I like it. It has a lot of potential but....it isn't quite as smooth as most of your other work. It looks like you may have to do some rewrites kiddo. By the way what happened at the end of your driveway? I had to park out alongside the highway and walk in."

Lisa propped her throbbing head on her hands. She looked up when she heard a heavy truck drive up. It was the tree remover. They had pulled the tree out of the driveway and moved her little BMW to the house. Two workers were busily pulling chain saws from the back of their truck. Soon the sound of saws working filled the air. Wood chips flew from the blades as the tree was reduced to small black sections easily handled. The men threw the pieces on the back of the truck and were on their way.

"I'm going to get my car and pull it up front. I'll be back in a few minutes," Beth pulled on a jacket and hurried out the door.

Lisa sank into the couch in the family area. She felt weary, tired and laid her head against the back cushions. Immediately things became different. Louis sat beside her his hand warm on hers.

"Are you all right honey? You look ill. Maybe you should put your feet up and rest." His face was lined with worry, his eyes full of concern.

"No! No! I don't want to sleep." Lisa pushed against him and tried to sit up. "I'm afraid to sleep!"

Louis leaned over her his hand firmly on her shoulder and tried to calm her, " Settle down sweetheart, it's all right. There's nothing to be frightened of...."

Pushing against his hands Lisa tried to turn away from him. Opening her eyes she found the worried look of Beth over her. "I don't know what kind of nightmares you're having kiddo, but things have gotten out of hand. I 'm going to insist you get some help."

Lisa sat up slowly and rubbed her throbbing head. Maybe Beth was right. She needed some answers as to why Louis only came to her in her dreams and why her dreams had become so terrifying.

Chapter Twelve

How long have you been seeing Louis?" the therapist asked. Settling into the couch more comfortably Lisa ran her hand over her eyes, "Since I woke up in the hospital the first time. However, it wasn't like it is now. Then he terrified me, horribly, until I regained some of my memory. Then he started coming to me in my dreams, as my lover, and I think as my husband. I found this ring one day in my bathroom." She held out the lovely diamond and gold ring for the doctor to see. "In my dream he slipped it on my finger and called me his wife."

Scratching on a note pad Dr. Brenda Allens make several notes then again turned to her new patient, "How long has it been since he last visited you?"

Lisa laughed nervously, "Last night. I can't go to sleep without him suddenly being there. I'm never afraid of him in my dreams, but lately our love-making has become uncomfortable."

"What do you mean?" Dr. Allens asked.

Lisa explained the session of lovemaking in the bath tub and how she'd had sensations of drowning. "Last night when he came to me he wanted to go for a drive with me, but I was too frightened to go. There's something about being in a moving car with him that scares the hell out of me." Sitting up she looked at the doctor, "What do you thing is wrong with me Doctor Allens ?"

Thoughtfully the doctor made more notes and then smiled at Lisa, "it's a little early to give you a diagnosis. However, you are on the verge of physical collapse probably because you are not sleeping correctly. That could be a large part of the problem. I'm going to give you some medication that will allow you to sleep without dreaming. You are going to feel groggy the next day, but should feel more relaxed. You shouldn't take this medication without having someone in the house with you. If the house were to catch fire you wouldn't hear the fire alarm. I'm only going to give you enough for three days. That should allow you to regain your strength. I'm also going to make another appointment for you to come back then. We'll see how things are going."

Beth stood up when Lisa came out to the waiting room. Explaining to her about the doctors orders she smiled at her friend, "I guess we're roomies for a few days then. Which shall it be....your place or mine?"

They decided Beth's house would be the better place to stay. "Topaz has his own room where I can close him up. He'll be fine and won't be throwing a hissy fit every time he sees you."

That night Lisa slept better than she had in months. She woke feeling rested but still groggy. Most of the day she laid around Beth's apartment resting but afraid to nap. By late evening she was anxious to take another pill. For the three days prescribed by the doctor things stayed pretty much the same. She could close her eyes without a sign of Louis. On the fourth day she again visited Dr. Allen...

"Well!" Dr. Allens exclaimed, "you look a lot better! I take it the medication worked and you were able to rest at night?" She opened her office door and let Lisa inside.

"Yes it did," Lisa admitted, "thank-you. I feel like a new woman." She took a chair across from the doctor.

"I think we're ready to head into the next step of your treatment. We need to find out what is behind these recurring dreams of yours. It could be repressed memory of a traumatic incident. I'd like to try hypnosis."

Quickly Lisa explained about her sessions in the Lewis county hospital with Dr. Langer and how ineffective they were. Dr. Allens frowned. "I thought I knew most of the psychiatrists in the Pacific Northwest, I don't know of Dr. Langer. But each doctor has their own techniques. I'd still like to try the hypnosis."

Lisa reluctantly agreed. Paging her secretary Dr. Allens told her to hold her calls for the next half an hour. "I'm going to ask your friend to step in here, if you don't mind. She may be able to help me once I get you under."

The lights were dimmed in the room and Lisa made herself comfortable on the couch. The only sound she could hear was Dr. Allens' soft voice. Following her instructions she felt her eyes becoming heavy with sleep. Relaxed and unafraid she drifted away on the sound of the doctor's voice.

He was waiting, sitting beside her on the couch and she smiled up at him tenderly, "Hi."

Sullen and cross he looked down at her and frowned. "What are you doing? Why are you here?"

Unable to see her dream partner the doctor and Beth watched with amazement as Lisa talked with her invisible lover. She didn't speak a word but from the expression on her face and the gestures she made they knew she was talking with someone. Softly Dr. Allens asked Lisa to tell them what was going on.

In her dream state Lisa heard a far away voice compelling her to tell what she was doing... With Louis beside her she began to describe what he was doing and saying to her... Suddenly Louis stood up, his blue eyes blazing with anger.

"I'll have no more of this! Lisa wake up!"

Her eyes popped open and she looked around the room, confused. Beside her sat Dr. Allens and Beth. Beth's hands were clenched tightly and held in front of her face as if she were afraid to speak.

Startled, Dr. Allens looked at Lisa closely, "Are you all right Ms. Miller? Why did you wake up?"

"I....I don't know! I thought you told me to." Rubbing her eyes she pulled her legs from the couch and sat up.

"No. I didn't. In fact I asked you to describe what you were experiencing…All you said was Louis was beside you and then you woke up. Do you remember what Louis said to you?"

Shaking her head she told the doctor no.

Dr. Allens frowned. "I guess we'd better quit for today, then. I want you to try sleeping tonight without any medication. It's important for you to get back into a normal sleep pattern as quickly as you can. A person can quickly become dependent on medication such as this. Take a long walk, be outside in the fresh air, do whatever you can to wear yourself out to help you sleep restfully tonight…"

Lisa and Beth thanked the doctor and stood up. Walking to the door the doctor laid her hand gently on Lisa's arm. "I want to see you again. I feel it's important to try to get to the bottom of this. If you have any more frightening dreams, we'll try again; the medication, the hypnosis, all right?"

Smiling, Lisa nodded and stepped outside the office.

Outside the building the sun was shining brightly. It was a short walk to the parking garage where Beth had parked her car but Lisa stood in the middle of the sidewalk for a moment looking around.

"Isn't Fred Norrise's office about four blocks up that way? " she pointed toward several tall buildings farther up the street.

"I think so," Beth answered and squinted in the direction Lisa was pointing…"Do you want me to drop you off there?"

"No. I think I'll walk. It's a nice day today. Fred called me a few days ago and asked if I could stop by his office some time to check out something he'd found. You go ahead and go back to your office." Giving Beth a quick hug she started walking, "I think I'll try sleeping at my own place tonight. I'll get a cab and pick up my car and things a little later. I'll call you tonight." With that she waved and quickened her pace.

It was farther than the four blocks she'd thought to Fred Norrise's office but it was a nice walk and she enjoyed being outside. The mid-afternoon sidewalks weren't overly crowded as most of the offices were still working…Finding the building where the Private Investigator had his office, she stepped into the cool interior and into an elevator. Getting off at the third floor, she was surprised to see Fred step out of his door and lock it behind him.

Looking up at her he smiled, "Ah, Ms. Miller! How are you today? You caught me on my way out to grab a bite to eat."

Lisa's stomach rumbled hungrily. She realized she'd not eaten all day and it was now close to three o'clock in the afternoon.

"Sounds like you could use a meal too. Why don't you join me? I know this little café not far from here." Grinning he led the way to the elevator.

Sidewalk tables covered in brightly colored tablecloths and matching parasols greeted the hungry twosome. Taking a seat it was only moments before a waiter appeared with tall glasses of citrus water and menus. Sipping on the water Lisa found what she wanted and waited for Fred to finish ordering.

While they waited for their food they chatted comfortably about life in the city; the cost of gasoline, how difficult it was to find a good dry cleaner and finally about Fred's business.

"I've always known I wanted to be a private detective. When I was a kid I spent most of my summers finding lost toys, lost pets, even lost keys for people all over my neighborhood. I loved it. When I graduated from high school I went to college and got a degree in law enforcement and even tried being a police officer for a while but I didn't like it. Too violent. Finally I applied for and won my private detective license and here I am." He stopped for a moment when their waiter brought their food. Digging in hungrily he chewed on his pasta dish while Lisa enjoyed her sandwich and salad.

"Do you find mostly lost people now?' Lisa asked as he sipped his drink...

"No. Actually most of my clients are corporations doing background checks on their newly hired employees or they've lost an important shipment or letter...Once in a while I get someone like yourself that has a lost loved one to be found...I must admit, those cases are the ones I enjoy the most." He smiled then, not a dazzling smile, but a warm comfortable one. "How' s your sandwich?"

"Delicious, thank-you." Lisa sipped her iced tea. "I didn 't realize how hungry I was until you mentioned eating. I'm sorry I barged in on your lunch."

"Nonsense," his smile was again genuine. "I get kind of lonesome…I don't have a secretary. I don't have any friends in the police department, like they show on TV detective shows. I don't have a cat or dog or girlfriend." He stopped obviously embarrassed, " sorry I didn't mean to say that."

Lisa smiled at his boyish behavior, "It's all right. You have to listen to all kinds of other people's problems. I don't mind if you want to talk about yours."

They finished their lunch with friendly chatter then. Paying their meal check Fred walked back to the table and helped Lisa to stand. "Listen, I don't want you to think I'm being crazy or anything but I've really enjoyed our time together and I kind of hate to see it end. I have some errands to run around town this afternoon. Would you care to go with me? I promise you I'll be a perfect gentleman and I'll take you anywhere you want to go whenever you say. Once we finish we can go back to the office and I'll show you what I've found."

Lisa didn't need any time to think about it. It was too pretty a day to be cooped up inside the apartment. She agreed to spend the afternoon with Fred.

The car Fred led her to was anything but in good condition. It was a 1976 Ford convertible, light blue in color. It smoked like an outdoor grill and rattled dangerously. At times it would stall and have to be restarted, but the two kept their sense of humor and laughed good naturedly whenever the car balked. Jokingly Fred told her, "My other car is in the shop….the pawn shop!"

Before the afternoon was over Lisa felt completely relaxed. She'd laughed at his jokes; listened to his stories; commiserated with his family loss; and enjoyed the afternoon immensely. She hated to see their time together come to an end.

It was almost seven when they finally made it back to the office. Letting them into the dark interior, Fred flipped a light switch and opened a filing cabinet. "I found this picture in an old newspaper when

I was investigating Julia Noles...It was taken at a small parade held in an Oregon border town. Take a look at it and tell me what you think."

In his hands he held a copy of a newspaper article with a large picture. It had been on the front page and had this caption, "Crowds of All Ages Enjoy Parade ". A woman held a little girl in her arms and pointed toward the floats passing in front of them. The woman's face was turned away and half hidden by the child, but the little girl, close to three, faced the camera, her finger to her lips, her little face puckered in a frown. Lisa had seen that same look on Frankie's face. The little girl looked like the photo she now carried in her purse; the one Dr. Mary had given her. It was her daughter Kelly, she was sure of it.

"When was this picture taken?" she asked softly.

"It was taken about four months after your little girl disappeared. The paper is printed in a small town on the Oregon-Washington boarder. I've never found any evidence that Julia ever had a driver's license. I figured the only way she could travel with Kelly would be by bus. It didn't cost much money and Astoria used to set along a major bus line. Unfortunately bus lines don't keep records of who buys bus tickets. I plan on traveling there in a few weeks. I thought I'd do a little nosing around." He took back the picture and carefully placed it back in a file.

"You aren't planning on driving your Ford there are you?" Lisa teased.

Fred turned a little red and ducked his head, "Yeah. Actually Old Blue is pretty reliable."

Shaking her head she told him, "You're nuts. Why don't I drive you? We can make a day of it. I promise you my car is more comfortable and reliable than Old Blue."

"But," he protested good naturedly, "I won't be able to charge you for traveling expenses!" Then he grinned. "Actually I appreciate the offer Lisa. I'll call you in a few weeks and we'll set this trip up."

Driving her to Beth's apartment Lisa retrieved her things. Beth had left a note on the refrigerator explaining she was having dinner with a client. She said she would call Lisa the next day. "Hope you sleep well."

Walking out to her car Fred whistled his approval. "Wow, a Beamer. Nice. I'm looking forward to our trip.....talk to you in a few days."

The trip back to her apartment was short and quiet. Images of the day kept slipping into her mind, making her smile. She felt good, tired, when she let herself in. Flipping on the light switch she was pleased to see the window had been repaired. Dropping her purse and keys on the table by the door she slipped out of her shoes and turned to her answering machine. There was only one message. Pushing the button she listened carefully, frowned and replayed it.

The voice crackled with static. "Lisa? Where are you? What are you doing? You should be home by now. I'll talk to you later...." the voice was soft but sounded disappointed, hurt, and almost angry. It was Louis.

She showered quickly preferring to stay out of bathtubs. Fixing herself a cup of hot chocolate she found a magazine and settled into her bed. Close to ten o'clock she turned off her light and nestled into her comforter. Yawning noisily she punched her pillow and closed her eyes.

"Are you asleep?" his voice was close and she opened her eyes wearily...

He laid beside her in bed, his face inches from hers on the snowy pillow slip. " Mmm, hi," she mumbled and stretched. "I'm sorry. I'm just really tired."

"Tired! You should be, chasing all over town with the PI guy you hired. What 's his name? Fred?" Louis turned over and looked up at the ceiling..."Did you enjoy yourself?"

Lisa also turned on her back and yawned again, "I hired him to find our daughter...He needed to run some errands and I went with him. My therapist said I needed to stay busy today, tire myself out....so I wouldn't dream...."

"About me?" His face was close to hers now and his blue eyes were blazing...His expression was one of hurt and anger. "Is that what she told you Lisa? Don't you realize this is all the time we can have together until....until...." he sat up then and looked over his shoulder at her. Frustrated he stood and started pulling his clothing on. "You don't seem to understand how important it is for you to remember, everything! There's no chance for us until you do!"

She could tell he was upset and she was sorry, but she was so tired, so weary. She had done nothing wrong, she knew that. He was over-reacting she told herself and again turned her head away. She heard her bedroom door shut noisily, yawned again and drifted into a peaceful sleep.

Chapter Thirteen

For nearly a month Louis stayed out of her dreams. Lisa felt and looked better than she had in a while. Able to sleep restfully at night she was full of pep and creative energy. Finishing the manuscript, including the rewrites Beth wanted, she handed her the hard copy, plus disc, and smiled.

"Wow! Are you a human dynamo or something?" Beth accepted her work and smiled at her. "Sit down for a minute Lisa. I haven't seen much of you lately. You look really good, what's been going on?"

Lisa laughed a little. "I'm not having any more frightening dreams. I've been working really hard, as you can see, and I've been seeing Fred almost every day. He and I run all over town most afternoons doing errands and cursing his silly car. I'm having a blast..."

"You're dating your private investigator?" Beth frowned at her friend. "Isn't that unethical or something?"

"I'm not dating him. I wouldn't call our relationship anything more than friendship. Since I've gotten to know him, I've found Fred to be warm, caring, energetic, honest and trustworthy. And a whole lot of fun," she looked at her hands a moment. "I just needed someone to hang out with, someone to help me quit thinking about all this other stuff. You know I love you as a sister and wouldn't do anything to hurt that. Do you think I'm really doing something wrong?"

Beth knew Lisa needed an honest answer and took her time thinking about what to say. Standing and walking to her second story office window she looked down on the public below her. "Since I've known you Lisa, now close to thirteen years, we have gotten really close and yet we've stayed pretty much out of each other's lives. I never offered, and you've never asked, for my opinion on your social life. Nor have I asked you for your opinion on mine. What you do is pretty much your own business." Lisa's face fell when Beth turned to look at her, "But! You must be doing something right. You look great, you're relaxed, happy, and your work is wonderful...I can't see that what you're doing is wrong at all."

"Thanks Beth," Lisa hugged her friend and then looked at her watch. "I have to go. Fred is going to take me to the newspaper morgue....he wants to show me some records he found not long ago. I'll call you tonight..."

Old Blue smoked its way to the long squat building that housed one of the local newspapers..."From what I understand this paper has been in publication for close to one hundred years," Fred explained as he parked the car. "It's been in this building for over sixty. Anyway, the basement of this place has a copy of every daily paper they ever published and distributed. They're on micro-film now for the public to view. I love going to this place." Fred held the door open and followed her inside.

Open space, the news room, humming with life, filled with desks. The atmosphere was charged with energy as people hurried to meet deadlines, to make last minute changes...Phones rang, keyboards clicked, footsteps hurried down aisle ways. There was a sense of urgency to the room. Fascinated Lisa stood staring at the heart of the newspaper.

Following Fred to an elevator she was shocked at the contrast of the lower floor to the news floor above. Below the hectic pace sat a gigantic press. Like the queen bee in a hive the workers scurried around it, adjusting, sampling, feeding the machine its life fluids. Before morning the monster would come to life, its spawn would travel around the town, the county the state. But now it lay silently, waiting for the switch that would bring it to life. Everything seemed hushed, subdued, as if the workers were allowing the beast to rest.

Fred led her into a brightly lit room that held several small machines used for viewing the micro-film. Seated beside him, Lisa watched and learned how to operate the viewers. Fred quickly accessed the information he wanted.

"Here's what I was telling you about. Remember the picture I showed you at the office? There's an accompanying story. In it the woman with the little girl refers to her as Janet K. If someone wanted a small child to change her name, wouldn't they just tack on another name to her own and possibly start calling the child by both names. A Marie would become Susan Marie and over time the Marie could be dropped. That child would then think her name was Susan..." Fred turned to Lisa. "That could have happened to Kelly. If Janet is really your daughter, Mrs. Napp could have started calling her Janet Kelly and then dropped the Kelly part. She would have grown up thinking her name is really Janet. After a while the parent could tell the child she was always called by that name and if young enough, the child wouldn't know otherwise..."

Punching a few keys, Fred scanned the information on the screen. "There' s something else you need to see. When you first hired me, you asked me also find out about Louis Sammons. I stumbled on something not long ago. I want you to take a look at this and tell me what you think."

In front of her was a short article, written four years earlier. The headline read, "Local Contractor Disappears Without Trace", her skin began to crawl as she read on;

Local law enforcement authorities are asking residents for any information they may have concerning the whereabouts of Louis T. Sammons. Mr. Sammons was reported missing by his long time partner, George Meyers. Mr. Meyers said Mr. Sammons was last seen three weeks ago when he left town in his late model Dodge pick-up for a business meeting.

Sammons, a paving contractor, was in the area completing a contract for the county road department when he suddenly went missing. A one time Idaho resident the authorities have contacted Idaho law officials but have learned Sammons has only one brother as his next of kin. Idaho officials have not had any success in locating his whereabouts...

Sammons drives a 1995 Dodge Ram. It is dark blue with silver trim. The license plates are Oregon issue, ZX 103. Anyone having information about Mr. Sammons should contact their local authorities....

Glaring out from the screen was a black and white picture of Louis. He was smiling and wearing a hard hat. Lisa turned away from the screen and looked at Fred, "That's him."

"Did you see the date on this article Lisa?" Fred asked softly.

The date read May 13, two years almost to the day, after she woke up in the Lewis County Hospital. "Maybe he decided he'd had enough of the contracting business and wanted to disappear for a while. His brother told me he' d done that once before, after he graduated from high school. He just didn't bother to contact any of his family or friends for years."

"Could be," Fred agreed. "I think it's odd, though, that he would walk out on his business partner. From what I've learned, he was considered by all of his friends and co-workers to be a very reliable worker. I've talked with Mr. Meyers. Louis has not tapped into his private bank account since he disappeared. As far as Meyers knows that's the only account Louis ever used. There was a large sum of money, over five thousand dollars, withdrawn the day before he disappeared, but that was the last transaction shown on his account."

"I'm confused," Lisa admitted as Fred turned off the machine and led her from the small room. "If Louis was reported missing two years before my accident, then why did he show up in my hospital room? He told me then he was a member of a highway crew and had found me after my accident. Maybe we should start there....find out who actually brought me to the hospital. I never thought to ask when I was there."

It was a silent trip back to Lisa's apartment building. Old Blue puffed blue smoke but did not stall or complain. Stopping at the front door, Fred turned to her. "Maybe we should go ahead and plan that trip to Astoria now and then go on to Lewis County. Will you be free to travel any time this week?"

Opening the car door she stood and looked down at Fred. "I just finished my work, short of any further rewrites Beth feels are needed, so I should be able to take off for a while. What about you?"

"I can be finished up with my other case by Wednesday. Shall we plan on leaving Thursday morning then?" He started Old Blue and looked up. " I'll see you in my office, bright and early, day after tomorrow." With a roar and a hiccup from his car, he was gone.

It turned unseasonably cool for September. By Thursday morning heaters were turned on in apartment buildings across the city. Vehicles left exhaust trails behind them and car windows were rolled up against the cold air. All over the city people were getting out their winter gear and gloves. Not quite to freezing, the unusual weather had people asking if winter would be early.

Lisa pulled up and stopped in front of the tall building where Fred's office was located. Feeding the parking meter she hurried inside. A brisk wind made the air feel much cooler than the 41 degrees reported on the bank reader board across the street. At the third floor she walked down the short hall to Fred' s office.

The outer office door was unlocked and she let herself in, but there was no sign of Fred. Taking a seat on the comfortable couch she waited. It wasn't long before she started to yawn. It had been hard to sleep last night, thinking about what they might find out once they reached Astoria and then on to Lewis County. Laying her head back against the cushions of the couch, she drifted off to sleep.

"Wake up honey." His voice was quiet. "We need to talk."

Sitting next to her was Louis. He seemed remorseful as he turned his intense blue eyes on her. "I hope you're not mad at me."

Smiling at him she gently touched his cheek, "No. I'm not mad. I've missed you. Where have you been?"

"That's not important. Let's get out of here, we can go back to your apartment and talk...."

The sound of the door opening made Lisa jump. Looking around she was surprised to find herself alone. Fred opened the door and came in. Smiling he set down his suitcase, "I forgot something and had to run home. I left the door open in case you came here before I got back. Are you ready?"

Following him downstairs to her car she opened the trunk for him. Once his suitcase was stowed she handed him a set of keys. "I never travel with just one set of keys and I always give my traveling companion a set so we don't get locked out. In fact, if you don't mind, I'd like for you to drive. I didn' t sleep very well last night. Do you mind?"

"Are you kidding?" Fred grinned, "I'd love to drive this jewel." He held the door for Lisa as she settled herself in the passenger's seat then skipped around to the driver's side. After adjusting the seat back and the steering wheel down, he slid the key into the ignition and started the quiet engine.

"Wow," he muttered as he slipped the car into gear and pulled out onto the empty streets.

Their morning was spent talking quietly about the countryside, the traffic, how well the car handled, and finally what they hoped to find once they reached Astoria.

"I thought we'd try the local schools first. If Janet was ever enrolled there should be some kind of record. Then we'll try the local health department. With Janice having been a nurse she would have kept the girl' s immunizations up to date. Then we'll check the hospitals to see if she worked." Spotting a large restaurant he pulled into the parking lot. "I don't know about you, but I'm hungry. How about some brunch?"

The restaurant was nearly empty. Ordering a quick meal of fruit and croissants they were back on the road within the half hour. Driving alongside the Columbia river the two remarked at the sights. Around them lush forest grew down to the road, vine maples put on a color display in readiness for autumn. The road twisted through low hills high above the river. Finally they reached the bustling port town of Astoria, Oregon.

It was early afternoon but they decided to get their rooms before pursuing their quest...Checking into a Super 8 Motel they freshened up then met in the lobby to make their plans.

First they would visit the grade school. If Janice had stayed in the area a few years, Janet would have been enrolled in kindergarten. Fred knew that Janet' s name had appeared on a school roster in Boise when she started the first grade...It was important to back track on Janice's trail as far as they could...

Looking at the somber building Fred turned off the main road and drove slowly up a short hill. "Did you know there was a popular movie filmed here many years ago?" He eased the white convertible toward the gray building. "Kindergarten Cop with Arnold Schwarzenegger was filmed in and around this school..."

Lisa nodded, she'd seen the movie once, thought it was charming. " Also one of the Ninja Turtle movies and the Goonies were filmed in this area." She added.

"I didn't know you were a movie buff," Fred said as he opened the door to the building. "Just one more thing we have in common."

Inside they went directly to the school office where they were met by the school principal...She'd been there for close to twenty years. "I'm sorry, but we don't keep records that long. In fact, all of our students move on to higher schools after the third grade. Their records go with them. Unfortunately we've only been using computer records for the last twelve years. But there is one way we may be able to help." She opened the door to a small room filled with photo albums. "We do keep photo records of all the children that have been enrolled here. We started this back in the fifties and as you can see our collection is quite extensive. The albums are in chronological order. If you like you can look through the albums to see if your daughter was ever enrolled here. These aren't the most accurate records, however. If a student was absent the day the pictures were taken often times we did not get their photo. What year would your daughter have been enrolled in kindergarten?"

"She turned six in February of 1983," Lisa answered.

Pulling a large album from the shelf, the Principal laid it on a small table. " Take as much time as you like. When you're done, just leave the album here. Good luck." she pulled the door shut behind her.

Lisa took a chair and began to carefully page through the album. Lots of little girls looked a lot like the picture she held in her hand, but there wasn't a photo of her daughter in the album. Sighing she closed the heavy book. "Is this the only elementary school in this town?"

Fred nodded.

"They must have moved before she started school," she said sadly.

Fred agreed. "I think our best bet now would be to go to the hospital in the area. Janice may have worked there for a time."

The office manager at the hospital wasn't very encouraging either. But she did make a suggestion that made sense, "Why don't you have DNA testing done? It'll prove whether or not the girl is your daughter."

Fred turned to Lisa with a comical apology written all over his face, "I didn 't think of that."

"You needn't feel foolish for not thinking about it," Mrs. Felding, the hospital nurse's supervisor said, "It's a new science that quickly became popular, especially in the law enforcement area. It is quite expensive to have the test done and it's hard for a lay person to find a lab to perform the test. And it takes a bit of time. If you do find a lab they' re generally booked for months before they can get to you."

Lisa thanked the woman and turned to leave. Fred silently walked behind her. "I'm truly sorry Lisa. I honestly never even thought about DNA testing…All that science stuff is new to me."

"It's all right Fred," Lisa assured him. "I didn't think of it either. I like to think I'm as well informed as the next person. Let's not fret over it. Let's just go back to the hotel and then tomorrow we can head on to Lewis County. Besides, I'm enjoying your company and we've been having a pretty good time....haven' t we?"

His smile was dazzling as he held the car door for her. "Yeah, I have to admit, we've been having a pretty good time."

Chapter Fourteen

The call to Janet was made that evening. On the other end of the line Lisa could hear Frankie giggling and playing with his daddy while his mom talked. "Oh Lisa! I'm so glad you called! I've been thinking a lot about you lately…"

"Me too, honey. How are you and your family getting along? How are you feeling ?" Lisa nestled into a chair while she talked to her young friend.

For several minutes they exchanged pleasantries, Janet telling her friend about her visit to the doctor's office. Now two and a half months along with her second child she reveled in hearing her unborn child's heartbeat. "I 'm feeling really good, except I'm a little tired. Frankie likes me to lay down with him in the afternoon and take a nap, so I'm coping…What are you up to?"

"I'm in Astoria, Oregon right now honey," Lisa said. "My private investigator and I thought we might find out something about Janice, but the trail has gone cold." The line was silent while Janet thought about that. "But a hospital director has made a suggestion that will put an end to the mystery. If you are willing, you and I can go in for DNA testing…The results will be positive proof if you are my daughter. What do you think ?"

Again there was silence. "I guess that's all right, but tell me something Lisa. If I'm not your daughter, will that change anything between us? "

Caught off guard by the question Lisa hemmed and haaed for a few moments. "No…Of course not. I'm going to love you and your family whatever the outcome of the tests. But, I would like to know what happened to my daughter. If she's the beautiful young woman who helped me get through the most difficult time of my life, then that would be even sweeter. If it's not you, I must keep searching for her."

Janet 's laugh filled the phone ear piece, "All right then. Tom has to be in Portland next week. Can we schedule the testing while we're there?"

Lisa explained she would try to get them a lab date. Then she asked if they would like to stay at the apartment with her while they were in town. Tom quickly agreed and they arranged to meet at the apartment on Tuesday.

"I'll stop at the store on our way over," Janet teased, "don't worry about meals."

It would be hard for Lisa to settle down that night. Fred asked her if she would join him in the dining room for supper. They ate a quiet meal, talked a little while and decided to leave early the next morning for Idaho.

"I hate traffic," Lisa admitted. "If you're still comfortable driving, you can continue to do so. It's kind of nice to let someone else sit in that seat."

Fred smiled and looked at his hands. "I do like driving your car. I've been looking for a new vehicle myself. I think when we get back I'll try to get something nicer than Old Blue."

"But it's so much fun to drive around in that old wreck!" Lisa protested…. "It has a personality all its own."

"I'd still drive it. Only a nut drives a beautiful new car around a crazy city like Portland." Then he realized what he'd said and blushed boyishly, "Oh! I'm sorry."

He can be so charming, Lisa thought to herself and smiled. "I agree. I don't drive my car that much in the city. I usually call a cab or walk."

A pianist was playing soft rock music in the dining room while they ate and a few couples were dancing on a small dance floor. Lisa looked at the couples wistfully. She couldn't remember the last time she'd waltzed or two-stepped. Across the table Fred must have understood the look of longing in her eyes.

Standing beside her he offered her his hand, "Shall we?"

It had been a while for both of them, but within moments they were moving stiffly around the small floor. They didn't talk, concentrating on where to put their feet, and keeping time to the music. It felt awkward at first but by the second song they'd gotten over their self-consciousness and were beginning to enjoy themselves.

Sitting out the faster songs they watched with humor while the younger members of the audience went through their gyrations. Fred ordered some drinks for them and they sat sipping their cocktails and watching the animated dancers in front of them. But when the music was softer they joined the small group on the floor. Smiling, laughing, teasing the evening turned into night. It was close to midnight when the pianist said this would be the last dance. It was a lovely old waltz, romantic and heart stirring.

Fred's arms felt strong and secure around her as their bodies moved with the beat...She could smell his cologne and her head swam with emotions fighting to surface...Perhaps the drinks have something to do with it, she told herself. She knew she was rather vulnerable right now. Fred felt safe to her, someone she could rely on when everything else was going crazy in her world. That could be part of it too, she told herself, she needed stability.

Afraid to look into his eyes she hid her face in his shoulder. Suddenly they were dancing closer to one another, barely moving. She felt him looking down at her and dared to steal a peek. His mouth was curled in a gentle smile, his eyes twinkled with affection. It felt so natural for him to pull her to him and kiss her right there on the dance floor.

Wordlessly they gathered their things and walked to their rooms, hand in hand. Standing at her door she found her key and he unlocked the door for her. Still silently they stood looking at each other, waiting for a cue as to their next step. It was awkward but sweet, their hesitancy to take the next step.

He lifted her chin and smiled, "Good night sweet Lisa. I'll see you early in the morning." His lips found hers and then she opened her door.

Confusion swarmed through her mind. She wanted to spend the night with Fred, and yet she knew she shouldn't. She didn't even know if she was a married woman, and if she was, where her husband was at. Fred was a man of honor. He wouldn't intrude on her privacy without an invitation. Sighing heavily she stepped into the bathroom and flipped on the light switch.

Gasping she stifled a scream and stood staring at the message on the mirror;

YOU MUST REMEMBER!

The unusual cold weather made its way out of the area and left the west coast with a glorious autumn day. The sun was warm, the sky clear and it promised to be a good day for travel. Fred carried their bags out to the car and stowed them in the trunk. Wordlessly he helped Lisa into the front seat and they started toward Idaho.

Exhausted Lisa said very little. She'd been unable to sleep all night long, the message glaring at her ominously every time she tried to close her eyes. Hardly able to think about anything else, she was anxious to get to Lewis County and get this trip over with.

Fred had frowned and grabbed both her arms when she told him of the message on her mirror the next morning. Softly he scolded her for not coming to get him. He was still having a hard time understanding who this Louis was. How could a so-called dream lover, someone that only came to her when she was asleep, manage to leave a message on a mirror? Could someone have followed them and then gotten into her room?

Lisa shook her head sadly, "No it's nothing like that. I don't know how he does it or why. But he must be around me always because no matter where I go, the messages follow. I really can't talk about it right now, Fred...Could you just get us on the road and get this trip over with?"

Bunching her coat as a pillow she tilted her seat back and closed her eyes. She was too tired to do anything more than sleep. Surely she could rest in the car without the danger of Louis showing up. Other than the time he'd rescued her in Jerome, he'd never been in a vehicle with her. Thus assured, she closed her eyes.

She woke once, when Fred pulled into a gas station to fill up. Preferring to stay in the car, she waited drowsily until she felt him beside her again.

It was mid-afternoon when they reached the Lewis County Hospital. Feeling a little more alert, and somewhat rested, Lisa suggested they find a motel for the night. She wanted to freshen up before they went to the hospital. Fred agreed and pulled into a Best Western motel alongside the road. Signing up for two rooms, she carried her small bag in and laid it on the bed. After she changed her clothes she started to redo her make-up. Standing in front of the mirror she looked down at the tube of lipstick in her hand. Wasn't this the same color as the one used on her mirror last night? There was no sign this tube had been used for anything but coloring her lips, but suddenly a thought occurred to her. Was she the one writing the messages? Could her subconscious mind be doing these terrifying things to herself?

Shaken at the thought, she threw the tube back into her small cosmetic bag and carried it outside to the car. Fred was leaning against the back fender waiting patiently for her. Wordlessly she opened the trunk and put her small cosmetic bag inside... Searching her purse she found a spare tube of lip color and threw it into the bag. Shutting the trunk she handed Fred her keys.

"What's going on Lisa?" he asked.

"I'm not taking any chances. I don't want to find any more messages on my mirror," she answered.

Opening the passenger door for her he drove them to the large hospital. He turned several times toward her as if to ask her a question, but didn't say a word.

Was he thinking the same thing? she wondered. Did he now suspect she was somehow causing this to happen to herself?

It was later than they thought when they reached the hospital. The main office closed at 4:30 and it was close to five when they arrived. But an admittance official was able to pull up her records on her computer.

Lisa had been found in the hospital parking lot. One of the secretaries remembered Lisa…"You were covered in mud and your clothes were soaking wet. You were dazed, unable to answer any questions at all. Dr. Priestly was on call that night…He did a quick examination of you and decided you'd been in some kind of accident. You must have been picked up by someone alongside the road and brought in then left in our parking lot. Not very chivalrous but a lot of people just don't want to get involved in someone else's problems. Later, the police found evidence that a vehicle had gone off the road into the Clearwater River outside of town, and divers found the vehicle. But no one ever knew how many people were in it. They just figured you had somehow gotten out before the car was slept away."

A shudder of terror went through Lisa as she thought of how awful it would be to be swept into a river like that. What a horrible way to die! Maybe that was part of the terrifying dreams she kept having, the narrow escape she'd had from that awful death. The sensations of drowning, her inability to breath, it made sense, sort of. But how had she gotten out of the water? She knew now she wasn't that strong of a swimmer. No one here could answer that question for her.

Dr. Priestly was not in the hospital that evening. He and his wife were on vacation and wouldn 't return until next month. There was probably little the doctor could tell them any way, Fred and Lisa both decided. Walking back out to the car, Fred suggested they drive by the river.

"Maybe returning to the scene of the accident will help you remember what happened," he suggested and pulled the car back onto the road.

The river snaked through the countryside, its gentle current and cool green water inviting a fishing hook or a skillful boater. Pulling into a rest area they watched as several children played alongside its banks, skipping rocks, pushing their twig and pine cone boats into the current. It was hard to believe such a tranquil stream could be that treacherous.

Driving farther up the road they reached the area described to them by the secretary. “It’s right by a large curve in the road. During wet or cold weather the roadway gets slick there. Three or four cars have gone into the river off of that curve. The highway department is in the process of redoing that part of the road so it’s kind of torn up right now.”

It wasn ‘t hard to find the right place. Not only was the pavement torn up, but alongside the roadbed where several warning signs. A speed limit of 25 mph slowed traffic even in the best of weather. A sign showing a swerving car headed toward a guard rail further explained the danger. Just looking at the slope of the road bed Fred realized how truly unsafe it was to drive on this road in a storm.

The river was narrower here and much deeper. The soft green color of the water was now a murky blue-green and the water swirled with little whirlpools and eddies. In the middle of the stream the fast current carried anything caught in its grasp quickly away.

Slowly they drove by the water. Suddenly Lisa gasped. In front of them, leaning at a precarious angle over the water, was a huge dark trunk of a dead tree. The snag sat alongside the river, had once been a lofty beauty. Now only the scarred carcass of the tree remained.

Pulling over onto a graveled area just beyond the tree Fred parked the car and hurried around to help Lisa out. She was trembling violently and leaned against him heavily...Unable to speak, her head was swimming with half remembered images. Inside her mind there was picture forming and it terrified her. Bracing herself against Fred she allowed the memories to return. Softly she began to tell him what she was seeing;

It was dark outside and the rain was coming down in sheets. Beside her was Louis...He was quiet, concentrating on the road ahead of them, but he was angry too. Around his eyes were lines of annoyance and a vein in his forehead was sticking out. They were arguing about something, she didn’t remember what, but they had spent the last several miles in angry disagreement.

He turned to her again and took his eyes off the road for a moment. Suddenly the truck started to sway, he grabbed the wheel and wrenched it hard trying to keep the truck on the road. Unfortunately he over corrected and the vehicle began to spin in the roadway. Lisa screamed as the vehicle slipped off the road headed for the swirling brown water. Sliding sideways it shuddered and came to rest against the dark tree trunk.

She had no idea how long she was unconscious. Her head had hit the frame around the window when the truck slid against the tree. When she woke up she was dazed…Stunned, she sat there for a while, unable to move. Louis was unconscious, his head was resting against the steering wheel beside him on the window, a smear of blood where his head had hit hard against the glass. Shakily Lisa looked around…Opening her door she looked straight down into the swirling flood water of the river. Shutting the door again she tried to shake Louis awake. Suddenly the vehicle began to slip toward the dark murky water. Terrified she screamed at Louis to wake up.

It happened so quickly she couldn't describe how fast the cab had filled with freezing brown water then somehow the window on her side of the truck cab had opened. At first her foot seemed caught on something and she had to struggle to escape but then she was out of the truck. Caught immediately by the current she was swept away by the river. Terrified, disoriented and unable to see, she was sure she was about to drown. Then her head hit a submerged log and she clung desperately to it. Eventually she was able to pull herself out of the water and stumbled onto the river bank. The pick-up was no where in sight, completely submerged by the inky black water. Crawling up the river bank she lay in the mud trying to catch her breath, gasping and choking until she lost consciousness. She vaguely remembered someone helping her into a car.

Describing what she remembered to Fred, Lisa was overcome with the terror the memory gave her. Her legs could no longer hold her weight and she found herself in his strong arms being carried back to the car. Sobbing uncontrollably she curled up in the passenger's seat and turned her head away from the horror of the river...

There were no words he could say to lessen the terror she was experiencing. Afraid for her sanity Fred carried her to her room and laid her on her bed but did not leave her side. She clung to him, his strength becoming her life line holding her from the brink of madness. Through the evening and night he held her, talking softly to her until finally the terror loosened its grip and she quieted. Toward midnight she drifted away into exhausted slumber.

Afraid to move Fred stayed beside her through the night. Pulling the blanket from under him he covered her and lay down beside her. He was unable to sleep.

This case puzzled him. It was obvious Lisa had undergone some kind of horrible experience...And it appeared she was being tormented by something; either a memory or maybe even a person. There was a certain vulnerability to her that he found endearing...This wasn't the first time he'd felt protective of her.

They'd spent a lot of time together these last few weeks. It had been a long time since he'd looked forward to being with someone just for the joy of their company. Lady friends of the past had been more of a physical attraction, a sexual need, than for the stimulation of a good argument over who had played the best Dracula in recent movies.

Their days had been spent in discovery of many different wonderments. A private garden filled with flowers had been a delightful afternoon. An offbeat restaurant where the food was all red, served on red plates, by waiters dressed in red and called the Passion Palace. Her smile and her quick laugh. All of these things made his long afternoons more pleasant. Was it just his loneliness that drew him to her or was there something more?

Pulling himself away from her he stood beside the bed looking at her. She was a few years older than he, she was an accomplished writer, and she was searching for a daughter fathered by a man that may or may not be dead. Walking around the room he tried to sort out all he knew about Lisa.

What if Louis hadn't died in that pick-up? What if he'd managed to escape his watery tomb like Lisa had? Was he stalking her? Fred rubbed his hands through his hair. That was a possibility. Lisa had escaped, possibly Louis had too. But why would he torment her? Was the man hiding from something?

And were Lisa and Louis really married? Fred didn't believe in them, but what if Louis was a ghost? A colleague of his insisted one of his clients had been haunted by his dead wife for years. She was jealous of her husband's new lover...

He needed a cup of coffee. Checking his watch he saw it was close to five in the morning...Lisa still slept soundly, not having moved for hours. He would slip out to the café across the road and be back in a few minutes. Using the bathroom he washed his hands and ran his fingers through his short hair. Satisfied he didn 't look like a bum, he shut off the light and looked again at Lisa. She was still asleep. Easing out of the door he hurried across the street.

When he returned she was still on the bed, having turned to her side but still asleep...In his hands he held a jumbo cup of coffee and a large sweet roll. This would hold him over until Lisa woke and they could have a decent breakfast. Seated at a small table in the room he began to eat his roll. Sipping his coffee he felt better by the time he finished, but his hands were sticky. Licking his fingers he walked to the bathroom and switched on the light.

The hair must have stood straight up when he saw the mirror. Written across it in lipstick were the ominous words;

COME TO ME MY LOVE!

Chapter Fifteen

Lisa knew nothing of the cryptic message on the mirror. Fred removed every trace of it before she woke up several hours later. Silently he searched the room for a tube of lipstick. He found nothing. While Lisa showered and changed her clothes he searched through her bag, still nothing. When he carried the suitcases out to the car, he checked her makeup bag still in the trunk and found both tubes of lipstick there. Puzzled he could not figure out how someone could have gotten into the room in the short time he was gone. He had the only key in his pocket. Things were getting complicated and just a little bit spooky.

Lisa was still shaky but her eyes were bright and alert. Turning to him her smile was bittersweet. "Thank you Fred, for everything. I guess now I know what happened. Louis must have drowned, that's the only answer that makes sense. For whatever reason his ghost wanted me to remember this accident. I'm sure I won't be troubled by him any more. Once the testing is done I'm confident the results will show Janet is my daughter. When we get back to your office I'll write a check....it looks like your work is done..."

He didn 't argue with her, not even when she said she wanted to drive. He sat silently on the passenger side of the car and watched the miles whiz by. He was forming a plan. His work wasn't anywhere near finished, in fact it was just starting.

It was harder to find a lab equipped to do the DNA testing than Lisa thought it would be. After making several calls she stumbled across an ad in the local paper. A new laboratory had just opened up. They advertised the ability to do all kinds of testing. Dialing the number listed she was quickly routed to the research department...

"I'm sorry ma'am but we're just not set up to handle cases like yours. Our lab is used exclusively by large research centers testing the DNA of bacteria. You need to call some of the universities in the area and see if any of them are equipped to handle what you need," the woman again apologized and hung up.

Discouraged but not ready to give up, Lisa looked up the number of three large colleges in the area. Two of them said they had nothing that could help her. Finally, she called OSU and was routed to the medical department. A Doctor Smith answered. Quickly Lisa explained her dilemma.

The doctor laughed good naturedly, "Sometimes trying to access new technologies and procedures can be a bit frustrating. I happen to know a small private college in the area that may be able to help you. As it happens they are gearing up for a new project. They're asking for volunteers from the community to give blood samples so the students can do research on them. I think they're planning on teaching courses in DNA fingerprinting. They should be able to help you. Just a moment and I'll get you the number of the professor in charge of the lab."

Finally after a day of reaching one dead end after another Lisa talked with Professor Walker and was told he would be glad to help her. If she and Janet could be there Wednesday afternoon, they would take their blood samples then. "Actually I'm quite excited about this project. We're hoping to establish ourselves as an accredited resource for this kind of testing. My students are very thorough but they are students just learning this procedure. We'll do the best we can but it could take several months to get the most accurate results."

Sighing, Lisa hung up the phone and called Janet back. Explaining what she'd found she told her, "all it will cost is our time and two vials of blood, each. The professor says he's not sure how long it will take.

This is a brand new procedure for this lab and well....not too many people at the college are trained to do this."

"There's no other lab that can do this?" Janet asked softly..."I mean, what good will it do us to have a test done if we' re not sure the results are going to be accurate? I want to find out as badly as you do Lisa, but I have my doubts."

Even though they felt discouraged they agreed to try the college lab. They would still continue investigating other leads. After hanging up Lisa called Fred' s number. Perhaps she'd been a little hasty in letting him go. There was still a spot in the world for old fashioned detective work. The phone rang about a half dozen times before the answering machine kicked on. Leaving a message asking him to call her back, she hung up.

At that moment Fred was looking out the window of a small plane. He was in a shuttle flight to Winnemucca, Nevada. From what Lisa had told him she may have eloped with Louis to some border town in Nevada. He would rent a car there and travel north to Denlo...He hoped with some luck and good detective work, he'd be able to find a copy of their wedding certificate. He'd tried on line to find the answer but there was no record of a marriage between Lisa Miller and Louis Sammons in the state records. He hoped searching the county records would give him a clue to look next.

Once he proved they were married, what then? He'd asked himself that question many times before. It was a place to start looking, he told himself, he' d just have to let his instincts take over after that.

Lisa combed her hair and pulled back the comforter on her bed. It was Sunday night and she was looking forward to a good night's sleep in her own bed. The incident on the river was still heavy on her mind, but it explained a few things to her. She was coping with it although it was hard to think Louis had lost his life. That made her feel sad and guilty.

Setting her alarm she climbed into her bed and picked up a magazine. There was a picture of a little blonde girl enjoying a fruity drink in one of the ads. She sat staring at the picture for a long time.

The years she'd lost with her daughter washed over her. There was an empty hollow feeling in her chest, a feeling of deep despair. She felt completely alone, there was no one for her now, no one at all.

A tear trickled down her cheek as she thought of how it could have been. Louis as her strong handsome husband helping her raise their beautiful little girl. And Kelly, little, blonde and petite. She would have grown up knowing the love of her Mommy and Daddy. She would have had sisters and brothers and lived in a beautiful home...Her own memories about the place in Adams were all good. Kelly would have had those same kinds of memories; climbing into bed with her parents on Sunday morning to read the comics; sitting in front of the fireplace on cold blustery nights roasting popcorn and marshmallows over the open flames; cuddling into her warm bed and knowing nothing could harm her in her world.

Turning her face into her pillow Lisa cried for all that had been lost. She was grieving over Louis, the lover of her youth and her husband of only a few days. She was grieving over a daughter she'd never had a chance to know. Wearily she sank into her bed. Closing her eyes she drifted away into a troubled sleep.

Holding a copy of the document in his hand Fred looked up and down the street before crossing it. It had only taken a few hours to locate the record he needed in the Winnemucca courthouse. Sometimes hunches paid off, he told himself.

It was late evening now, nearly eleven o'clock. He still had a two hour wait to catch the shuttle back to Portland. Maybe he'd better get something to eat, he told himself and yawned. Walking briskly across the street he headed to one of the many twenty-four hour cafes in the town. He could hardly wait to get back to Vancouver and show Lisa what he'd found.

"Honey, wake up." Louis' voice was close to her ear. She opened her eyes to his blue ones and saw his tender smile. "Hi."

Sobbing she wrapped her arms around him and cried against his shoulder. His kisses reassured her, told her it was all right. He tried to quiet her to get her to listen.

"Lisa, you need to hear what I have to say," he said quietly and pulled her arms from around his neck.

She reached for a tissue and wiped her nose. Tearfully she looked at him.

Taking her hand in his he kissed his fingers. "Darling you know about the accident, but you don't seem to realize what has really happened. Your survival of that accident wasn't suppose to be....we were suppose to be together forever. I've come back to help you understand how important it is for us....to be united."

"But you died in that accident," she sniffled.

Kissing her fingers again he turned to her with troubled eyes. "Yes, my love I did. I died trying to help you survive, but you weren't suppose to, you were intended to go with me. You escaped your fate, but that was wrong. But it's not too late, we can still be together."

"What are you saying?" she asked and pulled away from him. "I have to die?"

"You make it sound so gruesome darling," he said softly. " It isn't anything like that. There's a moment of discomfort, true, but then peace. Unbelievable peace. And freedom. There's nothing to hold you to the troubles and worries of your earthly life. It's wonderful Lisa...If it wasn't would I have come back to get you....my forever lover?"

Lisa hid her face in his shoulder, "I....I don't understand Louis. I just found Janet....she might be our daughter. We're suppose to go in for testing on Wednesday."

Louis smiled at her tenderly, "Under the circumstances do you think that wise ? If you are to leave this world then leaving her behind knowing she's your daughter might be unfair to her. You need to think about this carefully. If you won't be able to rest until you know for sure about her, then have the test done. But think how it will affect Janet. I've waited this long....I can wait a few days more."

His mouth found hers before she could protest. They clung together in a lover's embrace. His hands and hers sought the comfort of touch. Her skin began to yearn for his fingers and their lingering caresses. Before long she was caught up in a web of passion.

Rising from the bed he stood beside it. Looking down on her he smiled gently. He passed his hand over her face, "Sleep now darling. I will be back. I don't want you to be frightened. There is time, all of eternity, for us to be together...Rest now."

Her eyes became heavy right away. Sighing deeply she went to sleep.

Just returning from his rounds Bob made a notation in his log book and settled into a chair beside the reception desk. Pouring himself a cup of coffee he smiled. This job was heaven sent, he told himself. Good pay, good hours, and no hassles.

Sipping his coffee he frowned when he saw the elevator had been activated. He watched as it by-passed the lobby and went straight to the parking garage. Checking his watch he frowned. It was close to two-thirty in the morning. There were no guests signed in. All of the cars in the parking garage belonged to the tenants. Who could be up at this wee hour of the night?

"Might be Mrs. Blanchard taking that silly dog of hers outside. Damn little nuisance. I hope he doesn't leave a pile in the back garden again. I'll have to talk to the super about her." Looking at the log book he sipped his coffee again. Should he make a note of it in the log? Ah, hell. Let the super handle it. If someone complained, it wouldn't be hard to track down the four legged culprit.

As the doors to the elevator pulled open the dark man inside stayed in the shadows. Checking to make sure there was no one else around he stepped outside into the dimly lit garage. Walking quickly away from the elevator the tall dark figure slid the card lock into the slot beside the outside door and pushed it open. The breeze blowing straight off the water felt damp and cold. Pulling his jacket closer he jammed his hands into his pockets. Turning toward the vehicle parked several blocks down the street he quickened his pace.

He approached Fred at the Winnemucca airport and asked if he wanted to have a drink with him. "I'm not gay, you know, I'm just scared to death of flying...I hate to drink alone and I saw you purchase a ticket for the same flight I'm on. If you don't mind, could you have a drink or two with me, then make sure I get on the right flight?"

Fred looked down at the guy. He was a pathetic looking fellow, short, bald and had a huge nose. He was definitely scared, it showed in his eyes. And he was trembling. Fred felt sorry for him, reluctantly he agreed.

Thankfully the man held out his hand, "I'm Maynard Watson."

"Why do you fly if it scares you so?" Fred asked as they settled at the bar.

"Normally I drive, but I sold a large insurance policy to a young couple that were getting married soon," the stranger said and accepted a large drink from the bar-tender. "Instead of going through with the big wedding their parents had planned, they eloped the other day. Unfortunately they were in an accident on the way home and the young bride was killed. Any time we have large sums of money due to be paid on a premium, we investigate, especially if it's a new policy being paid out to a surviving spouse. And if that couple has only been married a few days, we get suspicious."

Fred nodded. As Maynard drank himself into oblivion he became more talkative. "We've had quite a few cases of fraud in the last ten years. Some of those that decide to do in their spouses get real creative. I heard about a guy that convinced his wife he was God and commanded her to drive her car into a river...Made it look like an accident too. The wife was kind of wacko to start with, but we thought there was something suspicious and investigated his claim. They'd been married for twenty years and everyone who knew them said they were crazy about each other. Even when the wife was showing signs of getting to be eccentric he took good care of her. But he had a gambling problem and was in debt up to his eyebrows. Her policy wouldn't pay big benefits for a death by natural causes, so he started working on her confused mind. He finally confessed, even told the investigating officers he didn't want his wife to suffer through althymers like her mother had and that he really loved his wife. But because of his obsession with gambling, he staged the accident. Now the guy is sitting in jail and if he gets out there's some shady underworld characters waiting for him."

Fred loaded Maynard on the plane and watched as he curled up into a ball and went to sleep. But what he'd told him made him think. Was it possible all of Lisa's problems were actually some kind of insurance scam? That would mean Louis was really alive and had to be living somewhere close by. And if he was living he was spending money. While the plane flew through the inky sky Fred sat thinking about different ways to track down the "ghostly" Louis.

Maynard smiled weakly when Fred woke him at the Portland airport. Stumbling off toward the taxi stands Fred watched as he climbed into a cab. "If you ever need anything, don't forget ole Maynard Watson, the best damn insurance salesman on the west coast." Shaking his hand he gave Fred his business card and drove away.

It was the wee hours of the morning when Fred found "Old Blue" where he'd left it. Unlocking the car he settled into the seat and turned on the engine. A cloud of blue smoke followed him out of the parking area and down the street. He needed to go to the office before he went home.

He was tempted to swing by Lisa's apartment building since he had to go within a few blocks of it anyway. But he knew he wouldn't be able to convince the guard he needed to talk to her right now. He decide his news would keep until morning. Besides, he didn't have much proof of what he suspected. Lucky ole Maynard the best damn insurance salesman in the world, hated to fly as much as he did. Fred chuckled, sometimes it paid to be a good listener.

Pulling up to a stop light, several blocks east of Lisa's apartment he waited for the light to change. Annoyed he listened to someone approaching at high speed...From down the block a large dark pick-up was traveling at a high rate of speed trying to beat the light about to change. Fred shook his head. Even at three in the morning there were bone heads on the road. He waited for the truck to pass by. As the large dark truck went under the street lights he could see into the cab. For a moment, just the slightest part of a second, Fred could have sworn he was looking at Louis. At least the pictures he'd seen of him looked a lot like the man behind the wheel.

Shaking his head he reasoned with himself, "I'm tired. I've been thinking about the guy all day. Of course I saw him." The tail lights were far ahead of him now and there was no way he was going to chase down a truck in the very early hours of the morning. Yawning he drove Old Blue to his office, locked the doors and went inside the quiet, dark building.

Chapter Sixteen

Lisa sounded subdued on the phone. Fred talked to her excitedly but she didn' t seem to understand what he was saying. Finally she interrupted. "I'm sorry I let you go. I need your help for a while longer. The lab I contacted isn't sure they can guarantee their results and I want you to keep searching for information on Janet."

"Lisa! You're not listening to me!" Fred scolded. "I found the chapel where you and Louis were married. I even found the Justice of the Peace that performed the ceremony. His wife was there that night and remembers you. She said you seemed upset and had probably been drinking heavily when you came in and the wife was worried the man was trying to bully you into marrying him. She tried to tell her husband but he didn't believe her. You were married two days before your accident."

"That only proves Louis and I are really married," Lisa said softly. "But I thought we'd already agreed on that."

"That's not the point," Fred continued. "It sounds like Louis may have been forcing you into this marriage. My question is, Why? That could also be what caused the argument between the two of you just before your accident." He waited for her to answer.

"Even if that's true, Fred, what difference does that make now? Louis is dead."

Fred had to bite back his quick answer. He wanted to tell her he thought Louis was probably still alive and living close by but he didn't have any proof, only suspicions...It would not do any good to tell her anything more. Her mind set was Louis was gone and she had to deal with that.

"Will you continue to search for any clues about my daughter?" Lisa asked tightly. "That's all I want you do. I'm satisfied with the information you gave me about my husband. If you're not willing to take the case of my missing daughter, then I will find someone who is." Her voice was quiet but sounded stressed and very unhappy.

"All right Lisa," he answered. "I'll keep searching for Kelly." Hanging up the phone he looked around his office. He was willing to bet everything he had there was a lot more to this case than what he'd uncovered so far. He'd go ahead with his promise to Lisa and keep searching for Kelly, but he'd do some snooping on his own. Louis was alive, he was sure of it and he would have to be close by. He needed to be where he could sneak into Lisa's life every once in a while....just to keep her off balance.

"But what is that bastard planning?" Fred asked himself. That was the part of the puzzle that didn't make sense to him. He tipped back in the seat of his chair. Recapping what he knew he went through the details of this strange case....Louis hadn't died in the accident but apparently convinced Lisa he had... Lisa had suffered from amnesia for months....Janet could be Lisa 's daughter....Louis' "ghost" was plaguing her at almost regular intervals. Why? What was it Louis really wanted? What was the missing piece?

There had to be more. Somehow he'd have to get Lisa to tell him what happens whenever Louis paid her a visit. He already knew about the lovemaking, but what else went on in that beautiful apartment of hers when her 'forever lover ' came to call?

Beth held the magazine in her hand trying to concentrate on an article but looked up when the door to the exam room opened. The doctor smiled at her and invited her in. "How have you been Beth? I haven't seen you for a while...You aren't still having trouble with anxiety are you?"

Taking a seat in front of Dr. Allens' desk she settled herself and smiled at her therapist. "Actually, Dr. Allens, I'm not here about myself...I'm here about Lisa Miller."

The doctor raised her eyebrows, pushed back in her chair and frowned. "I can't discuss someone else's case, you know that...."

"Oh no, I don't mean that," Beth interrupted. "I mean, I want your advice about Lisa. There's something weird going on and I don't know what I should do."

"Tell me what you've observed Beth, then maybe I can help."

Taking a deep breath Beth began to explain what she'd observed about her friend, "A few days ago I went to Lisa's apartment to drop off some papers for her. It had been two weeks since I'd last seen her. She didn 't answer the door, I had to let myself in. She was sitting in her living room, dressed in a robe, looking like hell. I tried to talk to her but she wouldn 't open up. I tried to get her to get dressed so we could go out to lunch, but she refused. She looks like she's not been eating."

Beth squirmed uneasily, "She kept looking out the window, would barely acknowledge I was there, and would hardly speak to me. As soon as I left her apartment I made an appointment to speak with you."

Dr. Allens stood up and walked to her window. With her back to Beth she asked if Lisa had mentioned doing anything to herself.

"No," Beth answered, "She didn't seem suicidal. She just seemed disinterested in everything. She was suppose to have some DNA testing done last week to see if a young lady is really her daughter. Lisa had seemed excited about it when I talked to her before. But Lisa called the day before they were to go to the lab and cancelled the appointment. She said she wasn' t feeling well and would have to reschedule. Janet called me that afternoon, concerned about her. When I tried to call Lisa all I got was her answering machine."

Dr. Allens turned slowly toward Beth. "Has she complained about any more visits from her ghost husband?"

"Not to me," Beth answered, "but lately she hasn't confided much to me."

The doctor sat down at her desk and looked at the worried friend. "I wish I could say there's nothing to worry about, but obviously there is. Lisa may just be preoccupied about something or undergoing some kind of stress. If she's suicidal there's some things you need to watch for," Dr...Allens removed her reading glasses and looked across her desk. "I'm probably breaking some ethics rules here, but I've been concerned about your friend too." Pulling out a file she opened it and scanned a page.

"Shortly after Lisa visited me the first time I did a little snooping and found out a little about her therapist in Lewiston, Elmer Langer. For one thing, he's not a doctor, he's a psychologist. Sometimes a psychologist takes the title of Doctor for his clients comfort. Mr. Langer has a dubious reputation, at best. He was once charged with unethical behavior when one of his patients committed suicide. The parents of the dead woman accused Mr. Langer of encouraging their daughter to end her life. The charges were dropped against him for lack of evidence. Right now, he's working out of a small office in Idaho."

"Dr. Priestly is Lisa's doctor of record, why would he bring in a guy like that?" Beth asked.

"I don't know Beth, and that's what has me worried. Lisa told us she'd been hypnotized a few times by Mr. Langer. It's possible he may have done her more harm than good in those sessions. That could be why I was unable to get her to open up to me. Until we know for sure, it would probably be a good idea to keep a close eye on your friend."

Dr. Allens took a seat and looked across the desk at Beth. "Your friend could be in real danger if someone has given her a subconscious, post-hypnotic command. That command would have to be reinforced from time to time, but that could be done in many ways, maybe even over the phone. If someone has planted a post-hypnotic suggestion they could trigger it with a single word...."

Fred picked up the card Maynard had given him at the airport and stared at it. Slowly he dialed the number. A secretary answered but routed his call right to Maynard..."Fred? What a pleasant surprise! Are you ready to talk about a policy for yourself?"

Fred chuckled, "No not at this time. You said I could call in a favor if I ever needed one, do you remember?"

Cautiously Maynard answered, "Yeah. I remember. What do you have in mind?"

"I'm a private investigator, and I need to know something. I don't need to know exactly how much or the whys or the where for but I do need to know if a Louis Sammons purchased an insurance policy on his wife, Lisa Miller-Sammons and if so, what date is on that policy. I have no idea what company he would have taken the policy through but it would probably be one that has offices on the west coast. I can give you an approximate date, May twelve of this year..." Fred waited. Would Maynard be able to help?

"How soon will you need this information?"

"As soon as possible. I know this is asking a lot but within the next few days would be great." Fred gripped a pencil so hard it broke, "I know you can access a data base that gives you that kind of information a lot easier than I can."

He heard a deep sigh and a quiet curse as Maynard came back on the line, "I knew my fear of flying was going to catch up to me one of these times....all right. I'll check. I'll get back to you as soon as I can....but if I ever need a private investigator...."

"Count on it!" Fred interjected.

They hung up. Fred had gleaned a promise from Maynard that he'd call back within the week, sooner if he found anything. Now came the hardest part of his job. The waiting.

To make the wait go faster Fred decided to spend a few nights watching Lisa's apartment building. He wasn't sure what he was hoping to find, but he was curious to know of the comings and goings of very late night or early morning guests. Packing his car with a thermos of coffee, sandwiches, and a special camera able to take pictures in poor light, he made his way to Lisa's apartment building at about ten o'clock that night.

Parking down the street he had a perfect view of the only doorway out of the parking garage... He knew anyone going through the lobby would be signed in or out of the visitor 's log. He could also see the automatic garage door. Checking his watch, he sighed. It was going to be a long night.

The first night only a handful of people left the building and that was all before twelve o'clock at night. The second night even less than that exited. He saw nothing unusual and was beginning to think this was a bad idea. Finally he convinced himself to try one more night. If nothing happened, he'd give up the idea.

It was close to three in the morning when he saw the dim crack of light from the garage floor entrance. He knew whoever was using that door had to have a special card key to get in or get out. Picking up his camera he trained it at the door and waited.

The figure of a man stepped out of the door and headed away from the building. He stopped to look up and down the deserted street. Fred's Old Blue and a vehicle parked three blocks away were the only cars in sight. The man was very tall, dressed in dark clothes and seemed to melt into the shadows. Fred quickly snapped several pictures and hoped for the best.

Laying the camera down Fred looked ahead of his car. He was pointed in the wrong direction to tail the guy, but two blocks down was a one way street that would allow him to turn and come up behind him. Waiting until the shadowy figure was half way to the parked truck, Fred turned the key in the ignition.

Old Blue let out a belch of blue smoke that echoed down the deserted street. The man, now nearly to his truck, turned toward the sound and watched as Fred pulled away from the building and headed farther down the street. Quickening his pace the man made his way to his truck before Fred turned the corner.

It was hard to keep the fast moving tail lights far enough in front of him to see where the pick-up was going and still not let the driver know he was being followed. He kept his lights on low beam, stayed blocks behind him, and almost lost him once... Finally the dark pick-up pulled into the parking lot of a small apartment complex... Fred turned off his lights and left the car running. Watching from the curb he saw the man climb the stairs to the apartment on the end and unlock the door. Making a note of the name of the complex, and the address he hurried home. Not bad, he told himself, for three days work.

It was early the next morning when he unlocked his office and picked up his phone book…Finding the number he wanted he quickly dialed it. A woman with a thick Hispanic accent answered on the second ring.

"Hallo? Who is this please?" she asked carefully.

"Oh, hello Senorita. My name is Sam Watson. I think an amigo of mine may be staying at your apartments. I saw a guy that looked a lot like him go into apartment number eight the other day. Does Richard Montgomery live in that apartment?"

"No, no Senor, he does not. Senor Robert Shriver lives there. I am sorry." Her voice was filled with an apology.

"Sorry to trouble you Senorita. Gracias and Adios."

Afraid to close her eyes, Lisa sat looking out the window. Beside her was a strong cup of tea. Sighing tiredly she picked up the cup and sipped it. Her head was swimming and her heart ached. She'd never faced a dilemma like this.

Louis had visited her nearly a half dozen times over the last two weeks. Each time he was gentle, caring, a loving husband, a good lover, and they had talked. Still convinced she should have joined him in death, he was now insisting she begin to think of ways of….doing it. "It will have to look like an accident, my love, so your friends and family won't be hurt…."

She couldn 't even think the words, she told herself and got up. Pacing her front room she looked down on the river below and shuddered. Beside her on the table her phone began to ring. She almost let the answering machine take a message, then sighed and picked up the receiver. After her cautious greeting, she heard a voice say one word, then nothing more. Setting the phone back down, she frowned…

Maybe she should go back to Adams. At least she was far away from water there. The old house might even calm her jangled nerves. The more she thought of it, the more excited she got until finally she turned to her bedroom. She could pack a few things, be on the road within the hour. She'd better call Beth and let her know, she thought to herself. If she didn't let Beth know what was going on she would alert every law enforcement agency between Portland and Adams that Lisa was missing.

Dialing her friend's home phone number she was glad when the answering machine picked up. She left a short message and hung up.

Pulling some under things from her lingerie drawer she stuffed them into an overnight bag...Throwing her cosmetic bag and a new pair of shoes into her overnight, she hurried into the bathroom to shower and change. It felt good to be moving around with a purpose. She was looking forward to being on the road.

The early September weather had turned unsettled. Grey storm clouds gathered above her as she turned her little white car onto the highway. Before her lay the road and miles and miles of thinking, but she felt excited about going back to her childhood home.

Pulling into a gas station she ordered the tank filled, then stepped into the snack bar inside. She bought a bottle of water and some hard candy. Picking up her cell phone she dialed two numbers. One of the numbers was Fred's, " I'm headed back to Adams," she told him. "I need time and space to think."

Hanging up she dialed the phone again, said a few words, then returned to her car. Paying the gas attendant she turned her car back onto the road.

Fred heard the message from the bathroom and hurried to pick up the phone before she hung up but reached for the phone just as she did. He'd been trying to get a hold of her for days. Not answering her phone and refusing to allow anyone to see her, he'd not been able to get through to her. Cursing softly he frowned and grabbed his coat. He knew where Adams was, had looked it up on the map. Maybe he could catch up to her, if she didn't drive too fast.

Grabbing papers off his desk he crammed them into a battered old briefcase. He needed to show her this evidence. She'd never believe him without it. Hurrying outside to Old Blue he threw the briefcase into the back seat. This was one time he wished he had a faster car, but prayed his old reliable wreck would be able to stand the strain. Turning the key in the ignition he checked his mirror and pulled out onto the street.

Music played softly on the stereo in the car as she headed east. Looking at the sky she frowned. Black clouds hung heavily overhead and filled the sky. Above her the threatening storm opened up. She switched on her windshield wipers and her lights and adjusted the defroster. Driving in the rain was not one of her favorite things.

Lightening crackled above her and the sky was lit with blue light as the storm worsened. The farther east she went, the higher the wind, the more rain. Finally she was pummeled with hail stones the size of marbles. They came out of the sky and bounced off her car and the pavement like popcorn. Maybe she should pull over until the storm passed, she told herself then shook her head. It was getting late and would soon be dark. She didn't want to be stranded out on this road at night...Besides, it was only a little thunder storm, she'd be all right if she kept moving.

An hour behind her Fred was having the same thoughts. Listening to the weather report on his ancient radio he frowned. A severe thunderstorm was pounding the area ahead of him. Old Blue was still chugging along and he blessed the old car. But he was afraid the old rag top would be damaged in the hail storm ahead. Deciding he 'd risk it, he kept going.

Listening to the message on his answering machine the man smiled a wide toothy smile. She 'd only said a few words, but they were enough. It was working, just like he'd been told it would. She'd never be able to remember making this call.

His blue eyes twinkled happily as he gathered his coat and headed back to his vehicle. This was great. She would be alone, away from her friends, who by now must think her ready to commit suicide. Things were progressing like they'd planned...

Pulling his large black pick-up onto the road he raced off toward Adams. He knew a short cut that should put him ahead of her. He had to get there before her for the allusion to be complete. Checking his mirrors he turned on a radar detector and sped off into the night.

With every mile the storm worsened until Lisa was straining to see through her flooded windshield. Afraid to stop, or to pull over, she slowed down and kept moving. Water was running off of everything. The ditches were full beside the road and at least an inch of water was moving across the highway. There would be flash floods, the radio told her. "No unnecessary travel, folks."

Lisa frowned and turned off the radio. That was all she needed right now. Straining to see through the windshield she could barely make out the markers alongside the road. The now familiar road held many landmarks for her that she could count off in her head. Ahead of her she knew there was a long curve and she thought she saw it coming up. Slowly she turned the wheel to her right. With a sudden jolt her wheels went into the ditch. High centered on the edge of the roadway her back wheels spun uselessly. She was stuck. Frustrated she slammed her fist against the steering wheel.

"This is just great!" she scolded herself. "Now what am I going to do?"

Looking around she decided not to get out of her car, unless she absolutely needed to. There were no houses in sight and she couldn't remember passing any in the last few miles. Her best bet was to stay where she was. At least she was warm and dry. After searching her handbag she was disappointed to find she' d left her cell phone at her apartment. She just have to turn on her hazard lights and hope a good Samaritan or a highway patrol officer would stop.

Only a few cars went past and they didn't stop. Lisa was growing more and more concerned. She'd been stranded for over an hour and now she was worried she'd have to wait out the storm before she was rescued. She still had over a half tank of gas, but it would probably not last her the night through. Thinking about the contents of her trunk she knew she had a lap blanket in there and she had her warm jacket in the car with her. She wouldn't be cold, at least, but she would probably be uncomfortable.

Just before she got to the point where she was ready to jump out of the car and pull the blanket from the trunk, someone's headlights pulled up behind her. Smiling, but cautiously relieved, she waited for her rescuer to approach the car...

"Hi Lisa, having some trouble?" his rugged face smiled from outside the glass. Water had flattened his brown hair and dripped off his nose. He reminded her of a wet dog. She'd never thought Fred looked better.

"Fred! What are you doing here? I mean I'm so glad to see you but I can't believe it's you! Get in out of the weather," she unlocked the doors and turned to him when he climbed in on the passenger's side..."This is wonderful. I was sitting here thinking no one was ever going to stop and afraid at the same time, that someone would."

Fred pulled out a handkerchief and wiped his face. "Actually I was hoping to catch up to you."

"Why?" Lisa asked and frowned. "I left a message on your answering machine explaining I wanted to be alone for a few days."

"I know, I heard it. But I've been trying to get a hold of you for almost a week now. I have some information you need to see....it's in Old Blue. When the rain slacks off a little I'd like you to come back to my car. I can then take you to the next city, and we can talk there."

Lisa said very little. She stared out at the rain flooded countryside. She knew she couldn't stay here in her car all night, but it irritated her to have Fred talk to her this way. "All right. When the rain lets up we'll get in Old Blue and you can drive me to Adams. It's about thirty miles ahead...But I'm going to hire a tow truck there and have my car pulled out of the ditch. Then I'm going home. Not to Vancouver, to my house in Adams..."

He'd left the lights off in the house when he went inside. He didn't want a chance passerby to notice someone was in the house, just in case there was an investigation later. Looking at the clock he frowned. He knew she couldn't be this far behind him, yet he'd been waiting for close to two hours now. Something must have happened. She might have gone off the road somewhere…

No doubt if she did have an accident, it wouldn't be a bad one, he told himself…She was too lucky for that!

Sullenly he pulled his coat on and headed back to the barn. His pick-up was hidden there, out of sight. He was soaking wet by the time he climbed into the cab and thoroughly angry. Starting the engine he left the lights off until he was on the road. With no one in sight he switched on his headlights and tore off back toward town. Surely he'd find her before long. But how would he explain this to her? Growling to himself he decided the time for explanations was over!

"I have the evidence Lisa, you have to believe me! Louis is not a ghost, he's alive and he's playing some kind of mind game on you." Fred looked deeply into Lisa's eyes. "Not only is he alive, but he lives about ten blocks from you in a ratty apartment complex and goes by the name of Robert Shriver. I've seen him, he's no ghost."

Her head was turned away from him but he could see how upset she was. But did she believe him?

Suddenly she turned to face him, "Why? Why is he doing this Fred? There's no benefit for him to do it! He can't touch anything of mine, I never changed my will, if something happens to me everything I own will be sold and the proceeds will go to my favorite charity."

"Not in the state of Washington. Community Property law. Half of everything you own, he automatically owns, according to state law. And if you die, he can put in a claim for all of it. All he has to show is a valid marriage certificate…But he's not just after your possessions Lisa. It's worse than that. " Fred pulled out a fax, "An acquaintance of mine, in the insurance business found a life insurance policy taken out on both of you by Louis. It's dated the day after your accident. While you were in the hospital trying to remember your life, your supposedly dead husband was taking out a two million dollar premium on your life!"

Stunned she stared at the paper in her hand. The rain was beginning to ease up a little but they sat there for a few minutes before Fred opened the door. "Come on Lisa, let's go back to Old Blue. We can drive to the next town and you can call this insurance guy if you want to."

Slowly she opened her car door and hurried to the hulk of the car behind them. Settling into the seat she asked Fred to get her things out of the trunk. She didn't want to take the chance someone would break into her car while it sat waiting for a tow truck.

While Fred scurried to empty the trunk she thought about what he'd told her. It made her feel....used....angry....upset. It seemed impossible to her that someone who supposedly cared as deeply about her as Louis apparently did, could do such a thing. And yet, she thought of the times lately when he'd talked to her about "being together forever...." he'd seemed impatient with her....didn't want to hear any arguments from her....was to quick to tell her there was no other way.

Ahead of her she could see Fred opening the trunk to her little white car. Across the highway she saw another vehicle approaching, a rather large pick-up truck. Seeing their plight the pick-up did a U turn and came up behind Old Blue. I hope that guy doesn't think he's going to pull my car out of the ditch, she thought. I'd rather the tow truck did it. Fred will explain to the guy, she told herself.

Pulling the trunk shut, with her overnight bag still in his hands, Fred walked behind his car to talk to the motorist that had stopped. In the rear view mirror Lisa could see the two men, their back to her, talking. Suddenly the motorist pulled out a gun and fired. Fred crumpled and fell to the ground.

Stifling a scream, Lisa watched with horror as the dark man approached Old Blue. Trembling with fear she was horrified when the man opened the driver's side and stuck his head inside the car. He smiled tightly at her, but there was no tender love in Louis' eyes now. There was only one thing on his mind, and it made her blood run cold.

Chapter Seventeen

There was no way Fred could know how long he laid there in the rain, unconscious. The first thing that came to his mind was, "My God! I've been shot!" Turning over carefully he felt the stab of pain in his left side. Sitting slowly up he pulled open his jacket and stared at the crimson stain.

Examining his side he was relieved to find the bullet had grazed him leaving a deep furrow along his side. How in the hell had that guy missed me? Fred wondered. Crawling to Old Blue's bumper he pulled himself to his feet and rested against the fender.

Slowly he worked his way to the front seat of the car and sat down carefully. His side burned like fire but it helped him stay alert. Lisa had said Adams was about thirty miles ahead. Hopefully he'd be able to find medical help there.

Curled up in the corner of the pick-up's seat Lisa stared with horror as Louis drove the truck down the highway at break neck speed. He was enraged and kept muttering to himself that all of his carefully laid plans were going to hell and now it was up to him to pull it all off.

By taking back roads he by-passed Adam. Turning the large truck toward the dark, empty house, he pulled up in front and stopped. Looking over at her he was irritated at her frightened expression. Mockingly he said, "Come on honey, we' re home."

She whimpered when he pulled the door open and carried her inside. Paralyzed by fear she crumpled into a chair. There was no escape for her now, she told herself. Her only hope had been Fred and now he was dying along side a country road with no traffic to stop and help him. A highway patrolman would find his lifeless body, but too late to help her. Sickened she looked at Louis. What had happened to make this man into such a monster and why was he doing this to her? Hadn't they been lovers as both teens and adults?

"I'm going to fix you some tea, honey." Louis said as he hurried toward the kitchen. "Just the way Dr. Mary used to fix it for mother. I left a pot of water on while I was gone. I won't be a minute. It will help you relax...." Walking into the kitchen he twisted his face into an evil smile. "Don't move. I'll be right back."

He was back in less than five minutes with a hot pot of tea. She could smell the aroma of the raspberries, lemon and honey and she knew there would be something in it that would put her to sleep. Determined not to open her mouth she decided to fight him with all she had.

But again she had underestimated him. He was as determined to get the tea into her as she was determined to keep it out. To make her cry out, he grabbed her breast and twisted it painfully, pouring a cup of hot tea into her mouth and clamped his hand over her mouth so she couldn't spit it out. Crying she fell away from him onto the couch.

"Why are you doing this?" she whimpered. "We loved each other once upon a time. We have a daughter...."

"Actually it has nothing to do with loving you," he answered tiredly..."It's about money. At one time I loved you more than life itself. But then my damnable brother tricked you and that ruined it for me. I know my mother was behind it, but don't you see, you were ruined. Even though I eventually found out the little girl is mine, I just couldn't stand it. I couldn't handle that he had touched you and kissed you like I once had."

He began to pace the room. "For years I thought about you and what mother had done to us. But I got past it. I became a successful contractor and my partner, George was proud of the work I did. But,

I deserved more money than he was willing to share with me. I started taking short cuts to shave expenses. Then I started gambling on some risky investments and my world crashed. I needed to disappear for a while to regroup."

"Those bad investments affected others. Isn't it ironic that Dr. Priestly and Mr. Langer were also involved in the same deal? They were hurting as badly as I was. That's when I had the idea of marrying my rich childhood sweetheart…If I could get you to marry me, by Washington law, I could legally tap into your accounts and bail my sorry butt out of a bad situation. But things didn' t go that easily. I thought we'd pick up where we'd left off over twenty years ago, but you were suspicious from the start. I was barely able to talk you into going on that trip with me. And I had to get you drunk to get you to marry me. When you found out I'd taken money from your account we quarreled and then we had that stupid accident. I almost drowned. I thought you had!"

Taking a seat next to her Lisa could see the desperation in his face. She was starting to feel dizzy.

"It was just meant to be Lisa. I mean it turned out so perfect. Dr. Priestly was on call that night and once I had a chance to talk to him alone, he agreed to help. Mr. Langer, or Dr. Langer as you know him, was a cinch. Between the two of them they came up with a plan to make you more cooperative. Between the hypnotic suggestions and the drugs they kept you confused and unsure. Then my part was to convince you I was your departed husband and convince you to come to me." He looked closely at her, "Ah, I see the tea is starting to work. You sit here honey, I'm going to run you a nice warm bath."

It seemed only moments before he was back. Sounds were coming to her now as if from far away. Sights were surrounded with a colorful aura and blinked in and out of a surreal plane. Weakened by the drugs Lisa was unable to fight him away. She felt him pull away her clothing and heard him sigh, "you really do have a beautiful body my love, I will miss it."

Carefully he carried her to the tub and lowered her into the warm water. "I guess I should have let Luke finish you off, but he was always messing up my life. I had to know it was done right and at the right time. There could be no question that it was an accident."

Seated on the side of the tub he stared down at her. By this time Lisa was seeing and hearing things as if all that was happening was wrapped in greasy cotton. Her mind was clouded, her sight was fuzzy and she was too weak to even try to climb out of the tub. Kissing the top of her head he told her, "I'm going to clean away my fingerprints my dear. It would never do for a ghost to leave prints. After they find your body a few days later I will emerge back into the world as Robert Shriver, also suffering from amnesia. Mr. Langer has it all worked out....how I can suddenly remember everything and claim the lost fortune from my deceased wife's estate. Good night honey. Sleep well. Forever..."

It was impossible to fight any longer. Her eyes rolled back into her head as she laid back against the cool porcelain and closed her eyes.

Dr. Mary examined his side and frowned, "You've been shot, but the bullet just grazed your side and missed penetrating your skin. You are lucky young man...Jim, hand me that roll of gauze there."

Fred winced as she cleaned his wound and bandaged him. "You should probably go to the hospital Mr. Norrise only it's an hour's drive away. You're lucky Jim works such ungodly hours or you wouldn't have been found until morning and a nasty infection could have taken hold." She smiled tersely, "I'm going to give you a tetanus hot and a shot of antibiotic...Then I want you to rest. You can lie down here for a while until we decide what to do with you. Tell me though why you had Lisa Miller's overnight bag with you."

"I'm the private investigator trying to find her daughter." Fred explained through clenched teeth. "She was heading to Adam tonight and I needed to show her some information when I found her car about thirty miles outside of town, stuck. She was still in her car. I was putting her things in my car when I was attacked. This guy, Louis, pulled a gun on me and shot me."

Fred groaned as the doctor helped him to lie down. "Lisa was headed to her house here. She said she wanted a quiet place to think."

Dr. Mary turned to Jim, "We'd better call the police…Jim, can you go get her car and tow it back to your shop before it's vandalized ?"

She turned back to Fred, "Do you know what Louis was driving? We'll have to give a description of his vehicle to the police."

Jim ducked his head, "Doc, it's gonna take the police about thirty minutes to get here. Maybe we should try to rescue Lisa our own selves."

Fred nodded, "I agree. But I think with Dr. Mary's help, I can help Lisa while you go get her car. I used to be a police officer so I have training and I don't want anyone else to get hurt."

Jim nodded and left the room. Dr. Mary helped Fred sit up. "I'm not sure I agree with this scheme but if what you've told us is true and it's Louis with her, we'd better get going. We'll take my car." Handing him a pill she told him to take it for the pain.

"I'll bring the car around to the front. Do you think you can make it out there on your own?"

He nodded…

Slowly, methodically, Louis went through the house wiping down everything he could have possibly touched. Satisfied he had at least smudged his fingerprints, he turned back to the bathroom. Opening the door he peeked inside.

Lisa was now sound asleep. She was laying on her side in the warm water. He'd given her at least three times the normal dose of sleeping tablets. When Dr. Priestly had given them to him he'd been warned how strong they were. She would sleep soundly for hours until she finally slipped below the water and drowned.

Unless her luck held out. He couldn't take that chance. Not again. This time he would have a back-up plan. Walking into the kitchen he blew out the pilot lights on the massive cook stove. Flipping each of the six burners on he covered his mouth as the smell of gas quickly filled the room.

Moving into her bedroom he lit the fireplace. The house was huge. It would take several minutes for the gas to reach the fireplace. Her bedroom was cozy and romantic. Looking around he remembered the many love making sessions he and Lisa had enjoyed here. At the time she'd thought him her ghostly lover, her forever lover...He smiled. Lisa was a sexy woman and she would be missed.

This was perfect. Fred's body would be discovered and everyone would assume Lisa had been kidnapped. They would assume she had been taken back here and killed for the money she had in her wallet. Easing out the front door he walked to his pick-up and parked it far up the driveway. Just to make sure, he'd wait for the outcome.

Dr. Mary drove her small car quickly toward the old Miller house. Beside her the private detective groaned every time he twisted too quickly or she hit a bump. " Are you all right Mr. Norrise? Maybe we should call the sheriff over in Lewis County..."

"No, I'm fine ma'am. Just a little tender. There isn't time to wait on someone else. I have a feeling we'd better hurry...How much farther to the house?"

"About another mile," she turned the wheel to kept from hitting a pot hole.

"Maybe you'd better tell me a little about the house. How is it laid out?" Fred asked.

"It's been a while since I've been to the house but from what I remember...." Dr. Mary described the inside of the house in detail. "Lisa's room is off the staircase. She has a double French door that open onto a patio that looks out into the orchard."

A break in the clouds above gave them a quick sight of the pick-up long before they pulled up to the house. Fred told Dr. Mary to turn off the lights before they were spotted...Pointing to an overgrown apple orchard sitting to the north of the house. "Pull over there."

"There's something going on in that house or he wouldn't still be sitting there waiting. I'm going to go in through the orchard. You wait here. No matter what happens, you wait. I'll be back as quickly as I can."

Pulling the cover off the dome light he disconnected the bulb then opened the door. Slipping into the darkness and the trees, he was out of Dr. Mary's sight in moments...

It was unbelievably dark. Although it was a full moon, the sky above was covered in clouds…Good thing I like carrots, Fred told himself as he hunched over and made his way through the trees. He was feeling a little unsteady, but steeled himself against the pain and dizziness. Spotting the doors on the north side of the house he waited until the clouds wouldn't give away his movements to slip up to the house…He tried the door. It was locked. Quickly he picked up a small rock and wrapped it in his jacket. Almost soundlessly he broke the pane next to the lock and let himself in.

It was dark in the room but the fireplace gave off a golden glow. Taking a moment to orient himself to the large room he spotted a door that must lead to the bathroom…Carefully he made his way to the door. Pushing it open he gasped.

Lisa's head was just starting to slip below the sudsy water. With one leap he was beside her and held her head above the water. Reaching for a towel he pulled her limp body from the water and wrapped her in it. Pulling a robe from the back of the door he slipped it on her and threw her over his shoulder. Making his way back into the bedroom he stopped. He could smell gas.

The hair stood up on the back of his head. Looking at the fireplace he gasped. Moving quickly he closed the French door and slid outside. Unable to see what Louis was doing he held his breath and moved quickly. He'd have to chance it. Moving through the shadows he cursed as he felt his side tear. There was no time, the house would blow any moment….

The sky was lit for miles with the orange ball of flame that erupted from the dark house…Afraid they would be spotted Fred dropped himself and Lisa to the ground. The pick-up sat less than a hundred yards away from where they lay. If Louis looked over this way, they'd be seen.

But Louis only smiled. No one could survive that blast, he assured himself. They would be lucky to find anything of Lisa to bury. Starting his pick-up he pulled out on the road and hurried back to civilization.

Dr. Mary cried out when the flames leapt into the sky. Fred had told her to wait here, but for how long? She saw the dark pick-up pull onto the road and head away from her. Suddenly she saw a small movement in the trees. Stepping out of the dark, Fred slipped Lisa's motionless body from his back.

She was beside them in an instant. Checking Lisa she saw she was asleep but otherwise unharmed. Turning to her patient she checked his side. "You' ve torn the wound Fred. You're going to need stitches." Reaching into her ever present black bag she handed him a gauze pad, "Put pressure on the wound to stop the bleeding while I get Lisa into the car."

Once Lisa was in the back seat, she helped Fred into the front. Taking a deep breath she turned to look at the fully ablaze house one more time before she started her car and hurried back to Adams.

The headlines across the state proclaimed the loss of the famous writer, Lisa Miller. Each article gave their account of the tragic explosion and fire, but all of them agreed, she had to have died in the holocaust. Her body was never found as the house burned completely to the ground. But evidence was found suggesting she was in the house at the time of the fire. Remains of her wallet, her house keys, and some jewelry...Sadly the literary world mourned her passing with cards and wires sent to her best friend and agent, Beth Mosher.

Beth looked at the basket of cards and wires beside her phone. It had been a week since the horrible accident had taken her friend's life. One card in particular was perplexing. It was from Fred Norrise, the private investigator. It had arrived this morning. In it he asked her to come to Adams as soon as she could. In it he claimed he was recovering from an accident and needed to show her something. Toying with the card she sighed and turned her attention to the yellow cat curled up in her lap.

"Well Topaz, I guess I'll be gone for a few days. You be a good cat and keep an eye on this place while I'm gone." Sniffing noisily she wiped her nose and went into her bedroom. Packing a small bag she decided it was a good idea to get away for a little while. She could get a room at the old hotel in Adams. And she admitted to herself, there was a morbid curiosity to see the remains of the house where her best friend had died. Wiping away a tear she picked up her overnight bag and went to her car.

It took most of the day for her to get to Adams, but it felt good to be out and away from the confusion of the city. Following the driving instructions in the card, Beth pulled up in front of a small house surrounded with a beautiful garden. Walking up the stone path she rang the door bell and waited. Inside she could hear a dog barking and feet scurrying around. Finally she heard, “Just a moment please, I’ll be right there.”

Lisa had described the good doctor perfectly to Beth many weeks before. Doctor Mary looked at her and smiled gently, “You must be Beth. Come inside dear, Fred is waiting to talk to you.”

Fred was lounging on the couch in the doctor’s front room. Grimacing as he stood he smiled at Beth, “I’m glad you came. Sit down. There ‘s something you need to know.”

“Who was at the front door? Is Beth here yet?”

The voice came from a back room but it was unmistakable. It was Lisa. Turning toward her friend Beth gasped and sat down hard. “Lisa! Oh my god Lisa! How is this possible?”

Lisa took her friend’s hand. “There was no other way to do this Beth…Fred, Doctor Mary and Jim are the only ones here that know. I’m hiding out until dear Louis makes his next move.

“Louis? I thought he was dead.” Beth said and accepted a cup of coffee with trembling hands. “Would someone please tell me what the hell is going on? Half the country is mourning your passing Lisa….and Janet. She’s in the hospital you know.”

Quietly she explained how Louis had deceived her, “Janet already knows Beth. We called her and let her in on all this the first night, before the news services got wind of the story. Tom suggested we put her in the hospital so the news reporters wouldn’t bother her. We couldn’t let you know any sooner, we needed you to act like you really mourned me. I’m sorry my friend, but you are not a very good actress and unless you thought I was actually dead, you ‘d never been able to pull this off.”

Beth was shocked into silence. Sipping her coffee she looked at the three people in front of her and frowned. "So what's the plan now? How can I help?"

Lisa smiled, "I knew we could depend on your help. Fred will explain."

Chapter Eighteen

Louis laid low for about a month. One morning an article appeared about a mystery man found living in the city. He claimed he couldn't remember his name, or anything about his life. He'd sought therapy when his dreams became terrifying and was discovered to be an amnesiac. His doctors, hoping to help identify this man, were appealing to the community.

"If anyone recognizes our John Doe, please contact us right away," and Dr. Priestly gave his phone number. A picture of Louis, smiling warily was shown next to the piece. All of the news wires carried the story.

George Meyer contacted the doctor right away. He'd been searching for Louis for close to two years, he told them. He had all the information about his former partner and the doctors listened with gratitude to all that he could tell them.

"May I see him?" George asked.

"He's at work right now," Dr. Priestly answered. " He's been working in a service station for almost three months. He calls himself Robert Shriver, but, if you want to drop by the station...."

George shook his head. What if Louis freaked out at the sight of him? No, he' d come back another time, if they needed him. He was thanked, again, and went on his way.

He'd found Louis, George told himself, but he certainly hadn't found any answers. A lot of problems had been discovered after his partner disappeared...His business was on the brink of ruin because of the way Louis had handled several jobs he'd been trusted to complete. Shaking his head George realized no court in the world would award him a lawsuit against a man suffering from amnesia...

Lisa's estate, the apartment, her furnishings, all of her investments were being held up in probate court while the judicial system sorted through her holdings. It would be several months before her estate could be settled, Beth was told. In the meantime, the apartment with all of its antique dishes was being catalogued for auction.

"Aren't you afraid of losing all your beautiful things?" Beth asked Lisa over the phone.

"Heavens no," Lisa laughed. "Since the accident I' ve lost interest in stuff like that. Let it all go if we have to Beth. But, I don't think Louis is going to stay lost much longer. I'll bet before the auction next week he'll remember everything."

Lisa was right. The auction was advertised with a picture of her next to the ad. "Auction of Famous Author's belongings. Antiques, household items, clothing, furniture...." the ad listed all that had been in Lisa' s world.

Smiling nervously she turned to Dr. Mary, "I hope he does something soon. This waiting is nerve racking."

The day after the ad appeared, he made his move.

Dr. Priestly was seen on local TV telling everyone how his patient had suddenly regained his memory after seeing a picture of his beloved wife in the paper. Robert Shriver was actually Louis Sammons, childhood sweetheart and husband of the famous author...Papers magically appeared showing they'd been married only a few days when the tragic accident had occurred wiping out both of their memories. Sadly Louis had not regained his memory before the horrible accident that took his wife 's life.

The world wept with Louis and shared his pain. Women all over the country wrote to him and offered to help him through these next few lonely weeks. The media followed his every move for days. As the news world moved on to other items of interest, Louis set himself up to move in on Lisa's fortune.

The courtroom filled up quickly with spectators. Probate courts don't usually hold that much interest to people, but this one did. Louis Sammons was laying claim to his wife's extensive estate. It looked pretty cut and dry to everyone in the room.

Toward the back of the audience gallery, Fred helped Lisa take a seat. She was dressed in dark clothes, wore sun glasses and a large hat. Not even Beth recognized her when she came into the room shortly after they did. Taking a seat next to Fred she smiled nervously.

"I made the calls, everything is set," Beth said lowly as she settled into her chair. "The prosecuting attorney we contacted still says this is pretty chancy. Louis has to incriminate himself otherwise his doctors can testify all that he did he can't remember doing and is not responsible. The District Attorney has let everyone concerned in on what's happening...."

Fred nodded and then shushed her.

The judge entered the court and seated himself. The Clerk of Court read the petition filed by Louis Sammons and heard the argument of Louis' lawyer. Facing destitution from the overwhelming costs of his medical care, Mr. Sammons asked the court to award him at least partial payment of his deceased wife's estate immediately...Frowning, the judge listened carefully. Looking at the attorney he asked if Ms. Miller's body had been found in the ruins of the house and why did everyone assume she had been there when it exploded?

"Ah, well sir," the lawyer stammered, "She left messages all over Vancouver telling everyone she knew she was going back to the house. Her car was found in a ditch about thirty miles away from the house. We believe she was probably picked up by a chance passerby and taken to her home, where later that night she died in that massive explosion."

"I see," the judge said then folded his hands in front of him. "Without her body, though, I'm reluctant to declare her dead, let alone grant this petition. Ms. Miller could be anywhere, could be anyone, could even be that woman in the back of the court room. Stand up please miss."

That was her cue. Standing slowly everyone turned to stare at the lady dressed in black with the black hat and dark glasses. It would have been comical watching the look on Louis' face had it not been so deadly serious. Removing her eye glasses and hat she stared into the shocked blue eyes of her husband and saw the horror...

Standing next to the table he pointed at her, "It....it can't be her! She died in that explosion....she died I tell you. I know she did...." He was backing slowly away from the lawyer who was trying to get him to shut up..."but you don't see, this is someone made to look like Lisa.... this is fraud....I know she died in that house....I just know it!"

The lawyer reached for Louis, trying to steady him, but Louis thought he was trying to grab him to make him be quiet and pushed away from him. Tripping over a cord laying on the floor he fell against a large oak pedestal table that had been pushed against a wall to steady it. Going to the floor everyone cried out when the heavy table teetered and fell across his chest. He wasn't moving when the bailiff pulled the table off and knelt beside him, and he was breathing either. Medical examiners would later tell them the table had crushed his chest and broken several ribs one of which pierced his heart.

Fate has a funny way of dealing out its own judgments.

It was a media circus for a while. Lisa's surprise resurrection in the courthouse was called everything from bad theatrics to a brilliant ploy of justice.

Standing beside Louis' grave Lisa tossed a rose down on the freshly turned earth and looked at Fred. "I really did love him at one time. I owed him a decent burial at least. Since the explosion I've remembered it all and I know now Louis was a very disturbed man."

Walking back to the car Lisa told Fred about the strange arrival of the flowers and the phone call so many months before. Louis had shown up on her doorstep ready to take up where they had left off twenty years before. "I was happy to see him, but I had a lot of mixed emotions about him. He'd deserted me when I needed him the most. I just didn't seem to be able to get around that..."

Holding the door of Old Blue for her Fred hurried around the car and slid in under the wheel. "I'm confused. If you felt that way, how did he talk you into going to Las Vegas with him?"

"I didn't have a clue what he was planning. He asked me if I would go with him for a week-end trip, just to get to know each other again. He said he'd found out some information about our missing daughter and would only tell me if I went with him. We could have separate rooms and everything would be above board. The next thing I know he's gotten me drunk and is taking me to a Wedding Chapel where it's all been set up. By then I figured he was desperate and dangerous and I was afraid to cross him. I went along with it, thinking as soon as I got back to Vancouver I'd have the marriage annulled....marriage under duress or some such thing. Then I found out he'd withdrawn a large sum of money from my account, using my bank card. We were arguing about that when the truck went into the river."

"What about all the warm and fuzzy dreams you were having about him?" Fred asked as he pulled the car into traffic.

Lisa turned her face away, "Ah yes....the dreams. My doctors at the hospital in Lewis County were behind that. Thanks to Dr. Allens I've been able to understand what they did to me. Dr. Priestly and Mr. Langer were actually able to hypnotize me and leave a post-hypnotic suggestion. Not only did I think Louis was the greatest man in heaven, but I was writing most of the messages I was finding on the mirrors. Evidently the post-hypnotic suggestions had to be reinforced periodically so they called every once in a while and said one or two key words and I would go under again. That way they kept the suggestions strong. They've confessed to everything for fear of being held on attempted murder charges. They claim they had no idea Louis was trying to kill me. They're in jail right now awaiting trial."

"I found a tube of lipstick in my overnight bag the other day, stuffed inside a tiny slit in the lining. And that's not all. Dr. Priestly gave Louis all kinds of drugs to use on me. And Mr. Langer gave him some kind of spray he could use to make me fall asleep instantly whenever he was ready to leave the house or my apartment. Evidently the smell of the spray was odorless to humans but my cat could smell it." She shook her head, "It makes me so angry! How could anyone do that kind of stuff to another person? I'm just lucky I have people who care so deeply about me…." she turned to face Fred and smiled shyly.

Fred felt his face flush as he drove toward her home. She didn't realize just how deeply he did care for her. But he knew this was not the time to tell her. He'd be patient. There was a lot more exploring for them to do in Old Blue and one day the setting would be perfect to tell her how he felt.

The DNA test results were as they hoped. Janet was Lisa's missing daughter, Kelly…Even the professor in charge of the testing was pleased with the positive results…It was a happy day for the two of them. Beth, Tom, Frankie and Fred were all at Lisa's apartment to celebrate.

Tom raised his glass of juice high and smiled wickedly at Lisa, "Do I get to start calling you Mom now?"

Lisa grinned and picked up Frankie. "I think that would be great."

Frankie smothered his new grandmother with chocolate covered kisses. Lisa smiled at her new family and nodded. "I think that would be wonderful," she whispered.

Fred pulled a document from inside his jacket pocket and set it in front of Janet and Tom. "A gift from your mother," he said softly.

Janet opened the paper and frowned. Handing it to Tom he did a double take and stared at the paper.

"What is this?" Janet asked, too shocked to believe her eyes.

"It's the insurance money from the policy Louis took on his life. When he signed the papers insuring me, he also insured himself. It's legitimate. I checked with my lawyer. We were actually married, and he signed the policy with only his name, before he could get me to sign mine. When he died he didn't name any beneficiaries, but the insurance company had a clause that said the money would go to the surviving spouse, me. I don't want any part of it. But I thought you kids might want it. You get the whole amount but not all at once. Over the next twenty years you'll receive a payment each year…You can spend the money any way you choose, start your own business if you wish…And there will still be enough left over to insure your children have a college fund. I figured if anyone deserved it, you two did."

Tom looked at Lisa with tears in his eyes. Janet snuggled against her husband and cried openly…"How can we ever thank you?" he asked quietly.

"Think of it as a gift from your mom and dad," Beth added softly and winked at the young couple.

Suddenly Janet sat upright and put her hand to her belly. Smiling she pulled Tom's hand under hers. Turning to Lisa she exclaimed, "The baby just moved!"

It was late when Lisa stood in front of the windows overlooking the river below. A large cruise ship was heading down river, and out to sea. No doubt there were dozens of couples standing on the decks looking up at this apartment building wondering about the people who lived there. Sighing she pulled the drapes shut and turned to face the large room. It was really a beautiful room, she again told herself…But it wasn't home to her anymore. She wanted space and grass and trees and flowers like what she had seen in Dr. Mary's garden and at the dark house. It was time to find another place, somewhere outside of town perhaps. Tomorrow she'd call a realtor friend and see what could be done with the apartment.

Apologizing to the owners of the house in Adams, they had assured her not to worry about it…"Actually the property is worth more to us now, then it was when the house was standing. There's a local farmer that has wanted the land for some time. He wants to replant the orchard. The house was heavily insured, dear, and we won't suffer that great a loss. The house was just too big for most buyers, afraid of the expense of heating in the winter and the upkeep. And most young people now days don't want to be that far out of town. We won't have any trouble selling the land now."

Dr. Mary had been as excited as Lisa when she found out Janet was really the long lost Kelly…Lisa felt lucky to have such wonderful friends. Without Mary's support she would never have made it through the weeks of waiting for Louis to make his move.

Touching her cheek she remembered the friendly kiss Fred had planted there when he said goodnight. A special bond had developed between them. She wondered if he knew how special he'd become to her. Over the weeks of hiding at Dr. Mary's house she had tended to Fred and gotten to know him quite well. Sickened by what Louis had done she was afraid she'd never trust another man. Fred had listened to her and helped her to realize how troubled Louis was. Now the very thought of Fred made her feel warm inside. She didn't want to scare him off by moving too fast, so she'd be patient. Maybe some time when they were out exploring the city in Old Blue she'd have the nerve to tell him.

Switching off the lights she moved into her bedroom. Turning down the bed she quickly changed into her nightclothes. Slipping into the sheets she turned off the light and yawned…It had been a long day but a happy day and she was tired and content. Yawning again she closed her eyes and drifted away.

He came to her in the night, his hands stirring fire on her flesh, his mouth tasting hers so gently, so sweetly. He wanted her, he whispered and slid his naked body next to hers in the cool sheets. She could feel his body hard against hers, warm and inviting and she turned eagerly to him. Her hands sought the comfort of his touch, his caress, his body and stirred with delight at each sensation. It was warm in the room and they kicked the blankets away….

Jerking upright she looked around the darkened room. A dream? she asked, and laid a trembling hand against her wildly beating chest. Sighing she nodded and laid back against the pillows. A dream, only a dream.

Smiling wickedly she turned to her side. She should be ashamed, she told herself, having those kinds of thoughts about someone. She wondered, for a long moment, how Fred would feel about her if he knew she was having such sexy dreams about him. But what harm could it do? she asked herself and snuggled deeper into her bed. Closing her eyes she smiled, It was after all, just a dream!

The End